Little Lost Things

By Mark Hill

Copyright

Table of Contents

Introduction

Every writer, no matter how talented they are, has unpublished work buried deep in the dark corners of their computer. Work that was too weird to find a buyer, work where one key problem could never be overcome, work that simply just wasn't good enough. I'm not terribly talented, so I have a lot of unsold work, and many of these works are short stories. Short stories are what first attracted me to writing, back when I was a teenager who had just discovered H.P. Lovecraft and decided that his goal in life was to become the next H.P. Lovecraft. The vast majority of my early work could be summed up as "Something terrible happens to a white dude with no personality, as described with far more syllables than necessary." One was about an evil chair, appropriately titled "The Chair." It's not in this collection.

What is in this collection is fourteen stories without much of a unifying theme beyond the fact that I'm not embarrassed to share them with the world, which is more than can be said for a lot of what I've written. There's science fiction and fantasy, horror and comedy, stories I think are pretty good and stories that are objectively not so hot but have a special place in my heart. There are two stories about magical snowstorms and two stories featuring drones, which are both at least one more than you're likely to find in most collections. A few have been published before, a couple more were bought but ultimately never used, some got me encouraging rejection letters, and others I never tried to sell, writing them only because there was a weird idea in my brain that would drive me crazy if I didn't let it out. They were written over sporadic late nights between 2011, when I started working in an office after university and was still learning how to string sentences together, and 2014, when I quit that job to become a full-time Internet comedy writer. They're my little lost things, found buried in a thick layer of virtual dust.

There's probably a few tpyos in here, because paying a professional editor hundreds of dollars to point out my failings would defeat the purpose of releasing a cheap, low-budget collection, and if you stare at your own work for too long you become blind to the little things. You do start to notice worrying trends when you're assembling a collection though, like your continued inability to give characters names that don't sound like they were ripped from the whitest people in my high school yearbook. A first draft of this collection had, like, seven Lisas. At the risk of further overhyping your purchase, I'll just say that these stories had a lot of loving hours put into them when they were first written, and a lot of begrudging hours put into them when they were being polished for this weird project. While that will make it all the more embarrassing when someone inevitably point outs that I got "than" and "then" mixed up like a complete amateur, hopefully it also means that I've produced something that will keep you entertained for a couple of hours. And I think that's all either of us can really ask for. Enjoy.

Heroic Deeds

"Look at that ass. Thinks he's so special." John frowned as Gerard the Great unveiled a statue of himself in the town square.

"Well, he sort of *is* special," said Robert.

"Oh, please. Just because he stopped one necromancer from annihilating the town it doesn't mean he's all that and a bag of oats."

"What, would you have rather he *didn't* stop Al'Kasamaresh? Someone had to destroy the ancient evils he unleashed."

"I'm grateful he destroyed the ancient evils. They were doing a number on my crops, and the howls of the damned were keeping me up all night. I just think he's taking advantage of the situation."

"I think you're jealous. How many necromancers have *you* stopped?"

"None, but that's not my job. *My* job is to slave away on the farm for twelve hours a day so people like Gerard don't starve to death."

Gerard was now being presented a ceremonial gold sword by the blacksmith. John rolled his eyes as the townsfolk cheered.

"Gerard was a farmer too. But that didn't stop him from answering his destiny."

"But that's just it, isn't it? The priests said the ancient prophecy foretold his victory over Al'Kasamaresh. If it was foretold, he would have won no matter what. He could have stumbled naked and drunk into Al'Kasamaresh's underground lair and waved his sword around until the necromancer walked into it, and it would have been destiny. 'Damnations, I've been beheaded by an errant drunkard! It's just as the prophecy warned!' It's bollocks, if you ask me."

"Nobody's asking you. And most people would spit in your eye if they heard you talk about Gerard like that."

"And that's what amazes me, that no one else sees this. Look, I get that he needed the Sword of Souls to complete his quest. Sure, it's a priceless artifact that's been in the town's possession since time immemorial, but you've got to behead a necromancer with something magical. Fair enough. But I refuse to believe he needed all of our other treasures too."

"Don't be ridiculous, John. He wouldn't have been able to stop Brogragg the Barbarian without the Ageless Axe."

"Why, what was wrong with the sword?"

The mayor was naming Gerard his honorary deputy. John spat on the ground.

"Well, maybe it… maybe he needed something bigger to behead Brogragg. Barbarians have thick necks, you know."

"But he never *showed* us Brogragg's head. And what about Malifagor the Magician? What did our precious Dwarven Diamond have to do with stopping him? Or Vamperious the Vampire and the Golden Horn? Did he kill Vamperious by rupturing his eardrums?"

"I suppose that isn't a traditional vampire slaying tool, but it worked, didn't it?"

"Or so he claimed. I wouldn't be suspicious if he brought any of our treasures back, but except for the sword every artifact's been 'lost in battle.' Then a week later he's paying the carpenter to add a room to his mansion."

"Come now, John, you don't think…"

"Oh, I do. Hells, he's not even trying anymore. I'm no expert on werewolves, but I'm pretty sure their weakness isn't 'the mystic power of a thousand gold pieces.' And when Wentilda the Witch showed up he claimed he needed to harness the magic of a virgin by spending a night with her."

"I don't see what's odd about that. Virgins *are* magical. Haven't you seen them around unicorns? I'd never have got my unicorn leather hat if it wasn't for virginal magic."

"Yes, but I don't think it's a coincidence that he said Ella the tavern girl had the strongest virginal magic in town. Ella, the beautiful girl that spurned his advances. And who hadn't been able to tame unicorns for years, if you catch my drift."

"Alright, so maybe he's taking advantage of the situation a bit. But hasn't he earned it, after all the horrors he's saved us from?"

As if on cue, the bard began the debut recital of his latest composition, a tribute to Gerard's victory over Wendrax the Warlock. John groaned as people began to dance.

"But why have we had so many bloody horrors in the first place? Before Gerard stopped the necromancer, we got nothing worse than the occasional lich. Now we can barely go a month without some monstrosity threatening to slaughter us all."

"So what, would you rather he *not* stop them?"

"Stop them from what, exactly? All they've done is kill a few chickens, tell some poor farmhand they're going to attack us, then wait for Gerard to come fight them. Pretty weak stuff compared to the necromancer zombifying our loved ones, setting them on fire and marching them into every wooden building in town."

"You scoff, but *I* was the poor farmhand who encountered Wendrax, and let me tell you, he was terrifying. He must have been at least six feet tall, with jet black hair, blood red eyes, and a deep voice that shook the ground itself."

"Just like the black hair, red eyes and deep voice of Brogragg, Malifagor, Vamperious, whatever the hells the werewolf was called, and even Wentilda the bloody Witch? Just like the black hair, red eyes and deep voice of Gerard's cousin, Steven?"

"Yes, just like them! You know, that's quite the… oh. Oh dear."

"Indeed. Don't bother telling anyone else, though. You'll just get, 'Ooh, But Brogragg's eyes were *pale* red,' or 'No, Vamperious' hair was *dark* black.' Dark black, Gods."

A scuffle had broken out over the right to dance with Gerard. It was resolved when the bard graciously agreed to repeat the ballad until every woman had a turn. John pretended to gag.

"I'm sick of heroes taking advantage of us common folk. Remember when we were children and King Kalim came to town?" he asked.

"Of course I remember! He rallied the entire kingdom against the Fallen Angel Satron and his orc hordes! It was the Battle of—"

"The Battle of the Ages, yes, yes. Now, remember that commoner he had with him? Matthew, the fellow whose destiny it was to strike the killing blow against Satron?"

"Aye, and strike it he did. Now there's a real hero!"

"But do you remember the speech King Kalim gave, about how it was *every* commoner's destiny to triumph in battle?"

"It was only the most stirring speech I've ever heard."

"It was so stirring that every man in town, including my father, was bursting with confidence when they marched off to war. Only nobody told dear old dad it was his 'destiny' to be sent out with a rusty sword and leather jerkin to serve as arrow fodder, while Kalim and Matthew fought in the reserves with fine elven blades from atop mighty white steeds."

"Oh, that must have been quite the inspiring sight."

"Aye, I'm sure dad was greatly inspired right up until he took six arrows to the face. You'd think if it was the most important battle in the history of man you'd have your blacksmiths spend less time making sure the dwarven armour of you and your honour guard matched, and more time making steel helmets for the troops. Hells, at least Satron gave *his* troops armour. Armour made from the bones of the women and children they ate, but still. Armour."

"Look, I know you're upset, but don't talk like that. Your father may have been underequipped, but it was still orcs that killed him."

"Do you know *why* they killed my poor father?"

"Because that's what orcs do. They kill people."

"Because they want land! We slaughter any orc that leaves the barren wasteland they're forced to call home, then label them evil when they get all uppity about it. I'd be evil too if I had to live in that hellhole."

"Why, that's just—"

"Oh Gods. It looks like Gerard the Great Big Dog's Cock is going to give a speech. I'll just go find a good place to vomit."

Gerard stood on the square's stone dais. Still flushed from all the dancing, he was nevertheless a noble sight—blonde hair waving in the wind, golden sword strapped to his waist and silver armour upon his chest. He drew the sword, which shone so bright in the noon sun that no man could look upon it. The townsfolk erupted in rapturous applause.

"Thank you, all of you. I may have been the one to slay the vile Wendrax, but I could not have done it without your support. Your love, and the beauty of this fair town, are what keeps me going in the darkest moments." Gerard's booming voice echoed around the square.

"That and all our treasure!" John could take no more, but his voice was barely heard over the thunderous approval of the crowd.

"Thank you. I'm humbled by your gratitude. *And* by this beautiful statue. Where's the gentleman who made it? He's the real hero, making me look that good in bronze!"

"We could have used that bronze for new farming equipment, you ass!" Robert tried to restrain John, but he broke free and hopped onto a barrel.

"While this battle was my toughest yet, I assure you all that I will be ready when the next threat emerges. And I—"

"Suck cocks!" John's heckling was now coming through loud and clear.

"And I swear on my life that—"

"I swear on my life that you're a twat!"

"Why, I believe the good farmer John has something to say!" The crowd hissed, but Gerard waved them silent.

"Now, now, he has the right to speak. That right is why I fight for all of you."

"You don't fight at all! You're a fraud, and I can prove it!"

"Now John, are you sure Wendrax didn't cast a spell of confusion on you?" Gerard grinned, and the people laughed uproariously.

"Don't patronise me, Gerard! I know—"

John was cut short by a rotten tomato. The hisses returned, and additional projectile produce forced him from his barrel. As he sputtered in anger, the hisses turned to gasps of shock. A blood-drenched farmhand had run into the square.

"Gods, boy, what happened to you?" asked Gerard.

"My chickens have been slaughtered, sir! A most vile man calling himself Bahlor the Blood Mage did the deed, and he swore to rain destruction on the town!"

"Can you describe this foul terror, boy?" said the mayor.

"Aye, sir. He was at least six feet tall, with pure black hair, dark red eyes and a voice that shook my very bones!"

"A most vile man, indeed! Can you stop him, Gerard?"

"I believe so. But defeating a Blood Mage will require magic of my own. The pure magic of nature, found in the very Earth itself."

"How can you acquire this magic?"

"Our crops, grown as they are by such righteous people, hold this magic. And no farmer here is more righteous than John."

"John! Dig up all your crops and give them to Gerard right away!"

John tried to speak, but no words came.

"Make haste, John," said Gerard. "I know you're too good of a man to ask for payment, especially since the town just bought all this bronze, but rest assured that you will have everyone's tremendous gratitude. Isn't that right?"

The townsfolk let out a mighty roar. Robert patted John on the back.

"You're right," said Robert. "He is an ass."

Family Photos

Jacob Smith was almost thirteen-years-old. Most boys his age would be awaiting presents and cake and a party with great impatience. But Jacob was not looking forward to those things. His impending birthday made him nervous.

He had no doubt his parents would buy him many nice presents and bake him a beautiful, delicious cake, as they had every year. They had even planned a big party, but his friends all made excuses not to come.

It wasn't that his friends disliked Jacob. It was his parents they didn't care for. They weren't sure why, for Jacob's parents were generous and kind and treated children with more respect than any other adults they knew. They were funny and clever, and never embarrassed Jacob in the ways all other parents embarrass their children. But Jacob's friends still didn't like his parents. They made his friends feel sad and scared for reasons they could never quite put into words.

Jacob didn't like his parents either. He knew that was a terrible thing for a boy to think, and it was even worse for a boy whose parents spoiled him with expensive toys and exotic vacations and all his favourite foods. But it was the truth. He didn't like his parents, no matter how hard he tried.

He especially didn't like his parents when it was almost his birthday. They would fiddle and fuss with his clothes and hair, and they wouldn't stop saying things like "Oh, look how big you've gotten!" and "Aren't you turning out to be a handsome young man?" It was enough to drive Jacob crazy.

Every week before Jacob's birthday his parents would dig out a camera from the basement, a camera so old it used film. They would put it on a large dusty tripod and take a family portrait. They would get the photo developed and add it to a brown leather scrapbook. The book had "Our Beautiful Jacob" written on the cover in gold print, and his parents would look at the old pictures and laugh and sigh and remember bygone days. Then they would put the scrapbook away for another year, in the top drawer of a locked steel cabinet in their bedroom.

Jacob thought it was odd his parents kept a locked steel cabinet in their bedroom. They said it would protect their most valued possessions if there was a fire or robbery. But all Jacob had ever seen them use it for was the scrapbook.

When Jacob's thirteenth birthday was just a week away his parents took another picture and brought down the scrapbook and oohed and aahed over it. Jacob did not join them in their journey through the years. He never did, and they never asked him to.

His parents had been even more enthusiastic than usual about this year's photo. They were so excited about adding it to the scrapbook that they forgot to put the camera and tripod back in the basement. It didn't look like they would tear themselves away from the book anytime soon, so Jacob picked up the tripod and put the camera around his neck and went to put them away himself.

Jacob's parents didn't like it when he went in the basement. That was fine with Jacob, because the basement was gloomy and musty and smelly. But if Jacob was going to be a good thirteen-year-old he had to brave gloomy and musty and smelly places, as well as ignore the wishes of his parents.

The basement had no light bulbs or windows, so Jacob took a flashlight. The light revealed an endless clutter of forgotten clothes and furniture and knickknacks that left little room to walk. As Jacob looked for a place to store the camera and tripod he saw old suitcases and a top hat and pocket watches. He saw a kilt and lace dresses and even a rusty sword. Everything was covered with dust. Jacob found it hard to breathe.

Finally, he found space between a stack of mouldy books and a big wooden trunk. Jacob put down the camera and the tripod and turned to leave, but stepped on something squishy. Jacob looked down and saw a cloth doll. It was much newer than anything else in the basement, and was the only toy. He picked it up and saw it had "Amy" written on a tag attached to the foot. He brought it upstairs.

His parents had put the scrapbook away for another year. When they saw Jacob had been in the basement a flicker of anger passed over their faces, but big smiles wiped their anger away so quickly that Jacob thought he might have imagined it.

His mother thanked him for putting away the camera, and his father said he had grown really strong if he could carry that heavy tripod all by himself. Jacob asked about the doll he had found. His mother said the family that lived in the house before them must have left if behind. His father laughed and said a doll was no toy for a strong young man, then took it away.

The doll reminded Jacob of other toys he had found in the house. When he was six he had crawled into a cupboard under the stairs and found a popgun, the kind a boy might have owned in the days when TV was black and white. And when he was nine he had pulled up a loose floorboard in his bedroom and found a pink plastic pony under it, a toy only a girl would play with.

He had shown both toys to his parents. His mother said the family that lived in the house before them must have forgotten them, and his father took them away. The cupboard was now boarded up, and the floorboard nailed down tight.

When Jacob was ten he asked Mrs. Glick, the old woman next door, what the last family that had been in Jacob's house was like. Mrs. Glick told Jacob that his parents had lived in that house for as long as she could remember, and she could remember back quite a long ways. Jacob told his parents what Mrs. Glick had said. They told Jacob that Mrs. Glick was very ill and very forgetful. He was told to stop visiting her so she could rest.

The day before Jacob's thirteenth birthday his parents went out, having promised they would return with a treat. Jacob had never been home alone. He had never even had a babysitter. His parents trusted no one but themselves to look after him.

Jacob went back to where he had found the doll. He tried to read the mouldy books, but they were written in a foreign language. He tried to look in the trunk, but it was locked. Jacob remembered the rusty sword, and used it to pry the trunk open.

It was full of dolls and plastic tea sets and stuffed animals and other toys for girls. Some had "Amy" scrawled on them in a child's writing. Jacob closed the trunk and went to his parents' bedroom.

Jacob rarely went in his parents' room. It was cold and dark and not at all what a parents' bedroom should feel like. But he was now very curious about what was inside. The steel cabinet was in the corner. It was taller than the dressers and wider than the bed. It was locked.

Jacob searched high and low for the key. He rooted through the dressers and the bedside tables and the closets in vain, and was about to give up. Then he saw that the family portrait on the wall, a blown-up version of last year's birthday photo, was uneven. Jacob removed the picture and found the key hanging on a peg behind it.

Jacob stood on the bed so he could reach the top drawer of the cabinet. The lock opened with a groan and a clunk. It took all of Jacob's strength to pull the drawer out. He took "Our Beautiful Jacob" out and flipped through it. In each of the thirteen photos Jacob looked different, but his parents had barely aged.

Beneath the scrapbook was another book called "Our Beautiful Amy." It had thirteen photos of his parents with a girl. His parents looked the same as they did in Jacob's book.

There were more books in the drawer. Jacob looked through "Our Beautiful Emily" and "Our Beautiful Felix" and "Our Beautiful Charlotte." They all had thirteen photos of his parents with a child. By the end of each book his parents looked a tiny bit older, but when a new book began they were young again.

Jacob opened the second drawer and found more books. In these the photos were black and white. His parents' clothes were old-fashioned, but their faces were the same. Jacob opened the other drawers and found books where the photos were grainy and scratched. He found books where the photos were on metal plates. In the bottom drawer the books contained portraits. His parents wore frills and wigs.

Jacob put all the books back. He locked the cabinet and put away the key and cleaned up the mess he had made. His parents returned just as he finished.

They had brought him his favourite meal from his favourite restaurant. He wasn't hungry, but he ate it all anyway. As he ate his parents beamed at him and told him how proud they were of him and how they couldn't wait to give him his birthday gifts. Jacob wanted to throw up.

He went straight to bed after supper. His father tucked him in and his mother kissed him on the forehead, and they both told him how much they loved him. When they left, Jacob took the knife he had snuck up from the kitchen table and scratched away some of his bedroom's blue paint. The paint beneath it was pink.

Jacob cried himself to sleep.

Jacob woke up on his thirteenth birthday to the sound of his mother and father knocking on his door. They told him it was time to get up, so he got out of bed and dressed. He sat on his bed and breathed deep breaths until he heard his mother's voice.

"Jacob? Come downstairs, sweetheart. Your father and I have a surprise for you!"

"I'm coming, mother." Jacob picked up the knife.

Spies Like Us

We went as far as the car would take us. I don't know exactly how far that was, because the odometer was broken. So was the speedometer, for that matter. What can I say? Crappy cars are easier to steal. It's not like there were any cops around to give us a ticket. We had a full tank of gas, but we were driving a real beater and keeping a guy tied up in your trunk weighs you down.

I do remember that it was nighttime. We got out into the country and God, there were so many stars. You forget about that, living in the city. When we ran out of gas we pulled over and sat on the hood like a couple of kids on a first date. We watched the stars and we watched the city. The skyline was beautiful on fire.

I held your mother's small hand in mine. Everything had gone to hell, but part of me was happy just to be alone with her. We forgot about you, asleep in the backseat. You were such a good girl. We forgot about the spy we had clubbed with a tire iron and tossed in the trunk like a load of groceries. It was just us alone in the night, hugging each other close when the cool breeze sent the corn fields rippling. I kissed her, and I wanted to stay in that moment forever.

We somehow fell asleep on the windshield, and I woke to the sound of you asking what the noise coming from the trunk was. I rolled over and immediately regretted it, my back aching like nothing I'd ever felt. And there you were in your little black pea coat. Sleep still in your eyes, teddy bear in hand, unaware or unconcerned that the world was ending.

I told you the car was broken. You asked where we were and what we were doing, and I didn't have an answer for that. So I told you to wake your mom while I made breakfast.

Cereal and fruit with a side of ash. The clock said it was morning but the sky was grey. The dust and dirt from the city blocked the sun. It got on our clothes and in our hair through a window that wouldn't roll up. But you didn't complain that it was in your food, that you had to have your Froot Loops with tiny pieces of buildings and people instead of milk. No, you were a good girl.

After breakfast your mother took you on a walk. She was looking for the farmhouse, for fuel and supplies, although of course she didn't tell you that. I watched the two of you walk into the grey hand in hand, and then I opened the trunk.

I eased the lid up with one hand while holding a pistol in the other. The man had worked through some of our hasty bonds, but he was still gagged and hooded. When I pulled him out he tried to stand but fell, stiff and weak from a cramped day and night. He sat on the ground, motionless. I removed the last of his restraints and sat across from him. I kept my gun trained on his head as he adjusted to the dim light.

He looked a lot like me, the same unassuming, forgettable look that so many of us have. We had been tracking him for months, your mother and I. We tracked him all across the city. He was good, and he was involved in something big. We didn't realise how big until we finally caught him, but by then the rods were falling.

So into the trunk he went. We told ourselves he was still useful, that our handlers would want to find out what he knew. And that was true. But I think there was an unspoken agreement between us that we didn't want him to escape with a quick death.

The man coughed. I rolled him a bottle of water, and he drank deep.

"So now what?" he asked.

"I don't know."

That was all we said until you two came back. I introduced the man as a hitchhiker in need of help. He raised an eyebrow at the sight of you, but said nothing. And you… you were just happy to meet new people. You were always happy to meet new people.

You told us all about the nice farmer, who gave you some candy and your mother a half-tank of gas. You told us about his cows and his chickens, and the cat he let you pet. You introduced yourself to the man, who smiled and shook your hand. You asked him why he was so battered and bruised, and he said he had been in an accident.

We drove. You got to sit in the front seat for the first time. You shouldn't have, you were still too young, but a traffic accident was the last thing on my mind. I told you it was a treat for your good behavior. I didn't mention that I needed to sit in the back so I could stick my gun through my jacket at your new friend.

We went as far as the car would take us again. It was slow going, driving through all that ash, but you didn't mind. You peppered your new friend with questions, and he was sporting in answering them. More than I would have been.

"How come you don't have a car?"

"I'm afraid I can't afford one."

"Do you have a job?"

"I used to. But I just lost it."

"How come?"

"Oh, let's just say someone wasn't happy with my performance."

"Where are you going?"

"Uh…" The man glanced at me, unsure of how much I had told her. I shook my head to say it wasn't much, and he nodded. I respected him for that. "A farm. To visit my brother."

"Does your brother have cows and chickens?"

"He sure does. Sheep too, and a couple dogs."

"I like dogs! Can I come play with them?"

"Well, that's up to your mom and dad." He looked at me again, smirking ever so slightly. I couldn't help but smirk back.

"Mom says her sister's really sick, and we need to go help her."

"Well, you probably shouldn't stop then. Maybe you can come on the way back. I hope she's okay."

"She'll be fine. You just worry about yourself," said your mom. She was less amused by the absurdity of the situation than I was.

"Do you have kids?" you asked.

"No, I… no. My brother does though, a boy about your age. I bet you'd get along."

"Does he like dogs?"

"Sure."

"We'd get along."

The man laughed, and he continued to keep you entertained as we drove. I just kept checking my phone, looking for a connection that I knew probably wasn't coming. As the battery dwindled I tried to resist, but it was a lonely road with a burning city behind us and nothing but ash ahead.

"Does your brother have ponies?"

"Stop bothering the poor man," said your mom.

"There's nothing else to do. This car ride is *boring*. Why is it still so dark out?"

"I don't mind," said the man. "I'm glad I can keep someone entertained. No ponies though, I'm afraid. I'll suggest it."

"Well, you won't have the chance for a while. This is the end of the line."

No more gas. Your mother barely got the clunker off the road. We stepped out into the cold. Christ, I don't know how the ash was still falling. At least it had thinned enough to let the dusk in.

"If you touch her or try to run I'll shoot you in the head," I whispered to the man, to no reaction. I took your mother aside, but we kept our eyes on the two of you as we spoke. Something he said made you giggle.

We agreed to make camp. We hoped that by morning the ash would have finally settled, and then... then we could do something else. We had sleeping bags, and enough food and water to last a few days. We wandered away from the road and found a little forest to shelter us from prying eyes. Your mother took you further in, promising to teach how you how to chop firewood.

"You've got to tell her sooner or later," said the man.

"Don't tell me how to raise my daughter."

"Sorry. It's just... the longer you wait, the harder it will be."

He sat and doodled in the dirt. I didn't even bother keeping my gun on him. He could have tried to overpower me, I guess, but where would he go?

The evening was quiet save for the sound of chopping. No birds, no distant farm animals, not even wind rustling the leaves. Just ash falling everywhere like silent rain.

"I didn't know," said the man.

"What?"

"That they'd drop the rods."

"Well what the hell did you think they were going to do?"

"I don't know. Not that."

"Saying you're sorry isn't going to fix anything."

"I didn't say I was sorry."

"Are you?"

"I don't know."

"What *do* you know?"

"I have friends there."

"Probably not anymore."

You came back with a little bundle of wood. As your mother got the fire started I took you aside and told you the truth, or at least a sanitised version of it. Our home had been attacked, and we were trying to find our friends. You nodded like you understood, or were good at pretending.

My phone buzzed when we were roasting marshmallows (the fact that your mother thought to bring them is one of the reasons I will always love her). I had a faint connection. I contacted our handlers, who gave us a time and a location. Tomorrow evening and a long walk from where we were. I begged them for more details, but the connection gave out and the battery soon followed.

You didn't notice me fiddling on my phone. You didn't even notice me throw it to the ground in frustration. You were entranced by the man, who was teaching you how to fold paper food wrappers into ponies. Your mother watched with a mixture of disapproval and bemusement. When the lesson was over she declared that it was bedtime and curled up next to you. The man waited until your eyes were closed to throw his pony into the dying fire.

When I was sure you were asleep I went back to the car and took out the bottle of whisky I had found in the glove compartment. I took a swig and offered it to the man, who accepted it without taking his eyes from the flames. Fresh ash flew up from them as the last lingering remnants of the city drifted down.

"There's a meeting tomorrow. You'll be debriefed," I said.

"That's a nice euphemism." He took a pull and passed the bottle back.

"Yeah, well, I'm sure you know a lot of polite words too. You better get some rest, it's going to be a long walk."

"You really think you'll make it? I'm surprised you haven't been swept up already."

"Were you surprised we caught you?" I took another sip and handed the bottle off again. Part of me just wanted to chug it.

The man laughed. "A little. I thought I was being so careful."

"You were. It took us a long time."

"Not long enough. So, are you going to tie me up, or are you just going to get me drunk?"

"I'm locking you in the trunk again."

"Aw, come on."

"I won't tie you up this time. And I'll give you water."

"I'd rather have the booze."

"I'll give you both."

"Well, have a little more to keep you warm first." He handed the bottle back. "What are you going to do about the girl?"

"What do you mean?"

"You can't win. You know that. Don't drag her down with you."

I thought of taking you from city to city, base to base, trying to stay one step ahead of the rods. I thought of you in a crowded camp or bunker, overlooked and underfed. And I thought of your bedroom, and the rubble it must have been by then.

"People like us don't just quit. You know that."

"I don't know. I think I will."

I put him in the trunk with water and the whisky and went to sleep.

I woke to your mother shouting something from deep in the trees. I couldn't understand her words, and then gunfire drowned them out. A couple of pops, staccato bursts, silence, a final pop. More shouts from new voices, then silence again.

It was dawn. The ash had been replaced by fog. The whole world was orange and grey. I remember the way the low sun caught your hair. It shimmered when you turned to me, fear and confusion in your eyes.

I hugged you with a gun in my hand, and put my finger on your lips when you started to speak. In that moment, crouched down in a cold, lonely strand of trees, I made a decision.

"Take this key, go to the car, open the trunk, and climb inside. The hitchhiker's in there. If anyone asks, he's your father. Do you understand?"

You didn't. I told you again, slower. I explained that the bad guys had caught us but he could keep you safe if you played pretend. I wished I had time to explain more.

I made you repeat my instructions. Then I gave you the key and my love and sent you on your way. I watched you go until you vanished into the fog.

I threw my gun down and waited. It didn't take long. The men were as polite as people who had just shot your wife could be.

The asked me a few questions there, and many more in their camp. They were very curious as to why I had one their spies and his daughter in my trunk. I told them it wasn't my car.

They gave me a relatively fair trial and twenty years in prison. The knocked off five years after the treaty, and took away another three for good behavior. They treated me well enough, though they could never tell me where they buried your mother. I doubt they buried her at all. After I got out I figured I could use my old connections to track you down pretty fast, and then you had to go and beat me to the punch. I guess he taught you a few tricks.

So that's the story, or at least my version of it. What happened to you?

What Happens in Japan...

"Look at that asshole. Sitting there like a big... asshole. 'Ooh, look at me, I'm Chad McCloud and I like putting testicles in my mouth!' That's what he should saying. The stupid idiot."

"Tell us how you really feel, Dave."

"I feel like you should get me another beer."

Dave put his empty on the table and shoved it away before he gave into the urge to fling it at Chad's head. His former best friend was holding court a few tables over, thrilling a dozen old classmates with yet another heavily embellished tale of battling the supernatural. Meanwhile, Dave was stuck at the Bestiary Club table.

He thought joining the club would make him popular. The world was being overrun by creatures of legend—who wouldn't want to know how to identity and fight them? Little did he know that his classmates would consider their very survival of secondary importance to the fact that "Bestiary" sounded like "Bestiality." It had taken him years to shake the rumours, and he would never shake the jokes. It didn't help that he had suggested the club motto: "We put our Best in the Beasts!"

"Get it yourself. You're just mad Amanda's hanging on his every word."

"Oh, shut up."

"Whatever. You know, you never did tell us why you started hating Chad. Usually when someone saves your life you act a little grateful."

"I was grateful he saved my life. I was less grateful about him telling the entire school every embarrassing detail."

"Come on, Dave. You have to admit the story's hilarious."

Dave disagreed. It was their senior year club trip to Japan, where they spent a month living with local families, attending a local school and studying the local monsters. Dave had almost been lured to his doom by a kitsune, a seductive fox-woman with ill-intentions. As ways to go out went, being fucked to death by a supernatural erotic temptress wasn't bad, especially for a lonely teenage boy. But

Dave preferred living, and he had been incredibly thankful when Chad saw through the creature's illusion and saved his life.

But Chad immediately began milking the story for all it was worth. It was one thing to brag about saving a friend's life—Dave could understand Chad seizing a chance to improve his social standing. But he didn't have to include parts that should have stayed between them, like the fact that the kitsune took the form of Amanda Powers, Dave's hopeless crush. And if that wasn't enough, Chad spiced up the story with a few choice lies, chief among them that the kitsune had made fun of Dave's tiny boner. By the time Chad was finished, he was a knight in shining armour and Dave was a hopeless, horny dunce.

Dave had decided not to call out Chad on his lies, because he truly did owe him his life. But now, as he watched Chad point at him, wave, and make a jerk-off motion while his table erupted in laughter, he couldn't think of a life decision he regretted more.

"You think so, Ben? Well how would you like to hear something even funnier?"

"Oh, this should be good."

"Shut it. Listen. Did you ever wonder why Chad omits the part that explains why we were wandering around the forest like a couple of clueless yokels?"

"Not really."

"You suck."

"Why does he omit the part that explains why you were wandering around the forest like a couple of clueless yokels, Dave?"

"I'm glad you asked, Ben. As you may remember, that was the week we spent in a rural village."

"Of course I remember. I went to the bathroom in the middle of the night and an Akaname was in there. Just… licking stuff."

Akanames were Japan's collective fear of nocturnal bathroom use personified. They snuck into dirty bathrooms in the dead of night to lick up the filth like the world's most disgusting maids.

"Wait, you saw an Akaname? What did you do?"

"I peed. It didn't mind. It just cleaned up when I missed."

"Dude, that's gross."

"I really had to go!"

"Well, at least you didn't ask an Aka Manto for yellow paper like Steve."

Ben laughed as Steve flipped them off from across the table.

"Hey, screw you, man. I panicked!"

Everyone in the club had encountered an Aka Manto. Another of Japan's bathroom haunters, this spirit asked people doing their business if they wanted red or blue paper. Red would make the Aka Manto slash you to death, while blue resulted in strangulation. The only way to survive unscathed was to decline the offer, although answering yellow would give you the non-lethal but incredibly gross result of having your head shoved in the toilet. For the Japanese, avoiding a horrific bathroom death had become as routine as washing their hands, but foreigners were required to be taught about Aka Mantos before entering the country. The shock of a nefarious spirit offering toilet paper sometimes overrode the training, but fatal incidents were rare.

"Whatever, shit-breath. Anyway, remember how everyone was invited to the village elder's house for dinner, but Chad was sick and I stayed behind to keep him company?"

"Yeah. Everyone assumed 'company' was code for 'butt sex.'"

"Wait, what? Seriously?"

"Yeah, man. You were young, pretty close, away from your friends and family in another country… it was the perfect time to experiment. Nothing wrong with it."

"That wasn't what we were… Jesus, never mind. Look, do you want to hear my story or not?"

"Does it turn out that the biggest monster of all was a cock monster named Dave?"

"No. Screw you."

"Alright, keep going."

"Chad had decided he was going to do a little extra-curricular work, even though our supervising teacher frowned on that sort of thing."

"Okay, that sounds *super* gay."

"You're the worst, Ben. Look, he had heard there was a Nuppeppō in the area. He wanted to study it and write about it for the club. And he wanted to keep the glory to himself."

"The glory of seeing a fat, stinky blob of flesh? Are you absolutely sure this isn't about your—"

"I am seriously going to cut you."

"Like your circumcised penis? That you put in Chad's mouth?"

"You know what? I'm telling this story to Steve now."

Their loud conversation had drawn the attention of the rest of the club, which was now following Dave's every word. Chad glanced over at their table, frowned, then went back to telling some bullshit story about fighting a chupacabra.

All the Besties knew about Nuppeppō. Ben's sarcasm aside, they were one of the reasons they had gone to Japan. Rare, harmless and hideous, the walking chunks of rotting flesh were little known to a world more interested in creatures that could murder them at a moment's notice. That was why no one had yet tested the legend that eating a Nuppeppō granted eternal youth. That, and the fact that doing so would essentially be an especially disgusting form of cannibalism.

"So, Steve, I brought Chad something hot to make him feel better, but—"

"Phrasing."

"*I am talking to Steve.* Steve, as I was saying, I brought him something, but he wasn't there. He was only playing sick so he could get a shot at the Nuppeppō. I looked outside and saw him entering the forest. I followed him, because obviously something was up."

"Phrasing!"

"Something *suspicious was happening.* And that forest was… well, you know the locals told us not to go in there, but they didn't tell us why. One step inside though, and you knew."

Dave shivered. It was years later, and memories of the place still haunted him. Twigs snapping beneath his feet, twisted branches blocking the sky, and the constant, lingering sense of unease. There was nothing strictly *wrong* with the forest, no obvious traps or threats. But you couldn't help but feel it was a place man wasn't meant to be.

"So I was following Chad, and Chad was following a Nuppeppō. Except when we got deep into the forest we discovered it wasn't a Nuppeppō. It was a Tanuki pretending to be one."

"A Tanuki?"

"Yup."

"Wait, so was it—"

"Yup."

"Seriously? With its…?"

"Yup."

A collective groan went up from the table, followed by peals of laughter.

"The Tanuki, for those of you who don't know, is a supernatural Japanese raccoon dog that's a master of shape shifting." Everyone in the Club knew exactly what a Tanuki was, but Dave was raising his voice for the benefit of Chad's table.

"While the Tanuki can shift forms completely, it often simply manipulates its 'golden jewels,' which can be turned into anything from an umbrella to a boat. In fact, there are some stories that say Tanukis can make entire rooms with their so-called golden jewels. Oh, hey Chad!"

A fake grin was plastered on Chad's face as he approached Dave. Chad's table watched with confusion and curiosity, while the Besties were torn between pity and glee.

"Hey, buddy. How's it going?"

"Good, good." Dave stood and shook Chad's hand. "You?"

"Good, man! What have you been up to?"

"Oh, not much. Just telling the gang about the time you chased a raccoon's testicles through the forest."

"Oh yeah, I uh… I forgot about that. What a crazy trip, right?"

"Yeah. Especially when you caught and tried to eat the testicles."

"Hey, look, maybe this isn't the best story to—"

"And then the testicles grew to your size and pinned you down. So you were stuck under a big ol' pair of hairy raccoon balls."

"Hey, Dave, come on—"

"And then all the other Tanuki came out, because you had stumbled across a Tanuki village. They had lured you there, because they had never seen a white guy and were curious."

"Dave—"

"And they made you sing and dance for them. And whenever they were unhappy with your performance they inflated their testicles to the size of beach balls and smacked you in the head."

"Alright, you've made your poi—"

"And then when you got angry and demanded they let you go they pinned you down again and took turns teabagging you."

"Christ, Dave, would you shut—"

"And then the elder, the one with the thick, luxurious, snow white ball hair, said it was time to let you go… but only after you massaged his testicles."

Chad's table had joined them, their confusion replaced by amusement. Other tables had drifted over too, eager to hear a new chapter in the saga of Chad and David. Chad himself was flushed red, from anger or embarrassment or both.

"And so you started working those huge balls. I mean you really *dug* in, got your hands and face right in there and rubbed every square inch of 'em. It looked like you were really into it. I mean, the Tanuki said it was the best massage he'd ever had."

"He didn't say—"

"And then they finally let you go, but not before every Tanuki rubbed its testicles on your head for good luck. And then when we got back that night your hair clearly had, uh, hair in it."

"Shut up already, you little—"

Chad was livid, but he was drowned out by all the laughter. Amanda in particular seemed to have found the story hilarious.

At the time Dave had thought about trying to rescue Chad, but concluded there was little he could do to fight or bargain with a community of supernatural raccoon dogs with magical testicles, especially if it came with the risk of getting giant animal balls to his face. The Tanuki didn't seem to have any truly malicious intentions, and besides, it would have made for a hilarious story to tell the Club later.

Not wanting Chad to realise he had been there, Dave snuck away as soon as the Tanuki let him go. He had almost made it back to the village when the kitsune appeared in the guise of Amanda. Tired and already confused by the night's events, he was ensnared before he remembered that Amanda was a continent away. Thankfully, Chad appeared before he could be spirited off, and in gratitude he had sworn to never tell a soul about witnessing Chad's embarrassing ordeal. Until tonight.

The laughter had finally died down, and Chad was looking to save some face. "Yeah, well, at least I didn't almost get myself killed trying to commit bestiality."

"Hey, I like beautiful women, and you like getting repeatedly slapped in the face with giant raccoon testicles. To each their own, buddy."

The laughter started up again. Amanda grinned at Dave, and he smiled back. Maybe this reunion wasn't going to be so bad after all.

Campaign Tactics

Evan laughed. He thought a Senator's daughter would be better educated in online security. But then you could always count on entitled teenagers to not take anything seriously.

Flora Welling's digital life poured onto Evan's screen. He had access to everything connected to her Universal ID. Facebook, Twitter, iSocial. Multiple email addresses. Accounts at Bank of America and Google Bank. She had impressive investments for a sixteen-year-old. Better than Evan's.

He took a sip of tea and glanced around the shop. Teens gossiped over coffee, self-proclaimed artists nursed wine and typed pretentious poetry, and university students wrote last minute papers in-between gulps of energy drinks. Evan wondered how many of them were also using the place for cover.

It was one of Flora's favourite haunts, so accessing her UID there raised no automated red flags. But he only had an hour before Flora finished dance practice and went back online. Even she wasn't ignorant enough to overlook a concurrent session alert. Evan took another sip and got to work.

He found the usual teen drama on her social networks. The odd case of bullying, a few private photos of her partying too hard. Evan saved a couple where she was obviously drunk, and another showing her popping some pills.

Her school account revealed bad grades and overdue homework, but no serious discipline problems. He had better luck in her messages. Nude pictures sent to her boyfriend, deleted from the sent folder but not the trash. He grinned. Careless.

Evan moved onto accounts separate from her UID. Sites that had refused to join the system, knowing their users valued their privacy. But with access to Flora's email it wasn't hard to connect the dots. He found a few racist comments on blogs and news articles. Accounts at fanfiction sites, where she wrote of thinly veiled stand-ins for herself getting swept off their feet by movie stars and boy band singers. Art site profiles, where she expressed an unusual degree of admiration for work featuring anthropomorphic dogs in suggestive situations. A *World of StarCraft* account, where she had acquired valuable items by using her feminine wiles on lonely players. Evan couldn't fault her for that. He had got some good loot that way himself.

Evan's time was almost up. He saved his findings on a flash drive, yanked it out and logged off. He shut down his laptop and savoured the rest of his drink. That was the easy part.

***

Another day, another coffee shop, this one for political professionals. Evan had swapped his scruffy student clothes for a sharp suit, combed his scraggly hair and removed his eyebrow piercing. He almost looked like he belonged.

He looked the place over as he added cream to his coffee. With the election around the corner, the mood was tense. The shop, normally bipartisan, had been taken over by Democrats. Last-minute strategies for close races were shot back and forth by stressed campaign workers.

He spotted his target at the bar. Russell Hargrave was sitting alone, working on a speech for Peter Hawke. The tech magnate was challenging Senator Welling in an ill-mannered contest too close to call.

Evan took the stool next to Hargrave and pretended to check his phone. Hargrave was too focused on his work to notice him. From his research, Evan knew that even at the best of times he focused too much on his work. He was a lonely man.

A cute young volunteer sat on Hargrave's other side. Evan coughed into his sleeve. She took her cue.

"Hey! It's Russell, right?"

"Yeah. Do I know you?" He barely looked up.

"We met at that fundraiser last week."

"Uh…"

"It's Sherry."

"Right, Sherry. Sorry, I'm terrible with names." Hargrave, embarrassed, gave her his full attention.

"It's okay! You must meet a ton of people. Although I thought I made an impression…" The girl pouted, and Evan rolled his eyes. She was overselling it.

"Oh, I'm sure you did! Sorry, I'm just a little stressed."

"I understand. It must be tough to work for a perfectionist like Mr. Hawke."

"You have no idea. Every speech I write comes back with about a thousand notes. Sometimes I wonder why he doesn't just write the damn things himself."

The girl giggled. "Well, I wish I could help, but I'm not much of a writer. I *could* buy you a fresh coffee, though. You look like you need one."

"Ah, you don't have to do that."

"No, but I'd like to." The girl batted her eyes. Evan had to suppress a groan.

"Well, okay. Sure."

"Then come with me! You're bad at remembering names, and I'm bad at remembering orders." The girl grabbed Hargrave's hand and pulled him towards the counter at the far end of the bar.

Evan took Hargrave's laptop and uploaded the files from the flash drive to Hargrave's UID storage. He checked the counter—the girl had Hargrave entranced. Evan grinned and opened Hargrave's UIM. Praying that Flora was sticking to her usual routine, he sent her a chat request. There was a long delay. Just as he was getting ready to abort, she accepted. He sighed in relief and started the conversation.

> R. Hargrave: Hello, Flora. How are you?
>
> F. Welling: do i know u?
>
> R. Hargrave: I'm an acquaintance of your mother. How's her campaign going? It's looking to be a very close election.
>
> F. Welling: its ok. what do u want with me?
>
> R. Hargrave: I wanted to talk to you about your behavior.
>
> F. Welling: my behavior?
>
> R. Hargrave: You've been doing things that are most unbecoming of a Senator's daughter, Ms. Welling. Getting drunk, doing drugs, exposing yourself for the camera…
>
> F. Welling: i dont know what ur talking about
>
> R. Hargrave: Oh, I think you do. Unless you don't remember taking this?

Evan sent a link to one of her nudes.

> F. Welling: how the hell did u get that??

R. Hargrave: Oh, that's not important. What is important is that I haven't made it public. Yet.

F. Welling: u perv! why would u do that?

R. Hargrave: Your mother's core supporters are strong believers in "family values." How do you think they'll react when they learn the daughter of their prim and proper Senator is a drunken amateur pornographer with a penchant for perverted artwork and fanfic?

F. Welling: r u trying to blackmail me? i'm not giving u money

R. Hargrave: I didn't say anything about blackmail. I'd just like you to let your mother know that I'm in the possession of some interesting personal information. What she does with that knowledge is up to her.

F. Welling: lol, your trying to blackmail my mom? how dumb r u?

R. Hargrave: I beg your pardon?

F. Welling: my mom used to be a lawyer, dude. u send that shit to anyone and she'll bust ur ass for child porn or something

R. Hargrave: We'll see about that. Good day, Ms. Welling.

Evan logged out of Hargrave's UIM, slipped the flash drive into the man's bag and left the shop.

***

Evan went to a new coffee shop the next day. Also for political types, this one had become a Republican stronghold. He watched CNN on his laptop, a live report on Russell Hargrave's attempt to blackmail Senator Welling's daughter. The scandal had sent Peter Hawke's poll numbers into free-fall. A woman sat next to him. He didn't look up.

"That was a hell of a gamble," said Evan.

"Eh, the blackmail angle's juicier than a story about a wild teenage girl. And the Senator has good legal and media connections. It was a calculated risk."

"Do you think the charges will stick? I'd feel kinda bad if the guy went to jail."

"I doubt it, but the election will be over by the time it clears up. It doesn't matter anyway, as long as you were smart enough to cover your tracks."

"Obviously. You going to tell the Senator about your little scheme? It looks like it will win her the election."

"Hell no. You going to vote for her?"

"Hell no."

"Fair enough." The woman put an envelope on the bar and left.

Evan pocketed it, appreciating the irony of being paid with physical cash. Then he closed the news feed and started working. The word from his next client was that Microsoft's new CEO had bad security habits and interesting fetishes.

Summer Snow

It was snowing in September. Lisa opened the window and listened to the thick flakes rustling through the trees. The world was whispering.

"Lisa, close the window! It's freezing out."

"Sorry, mom."

Lisa went to the closet and dug out her winter coat. She put it on and slipped on her sandals and snuck out the back door.

Her mother was exaggerating. With her coat on it was barely cold at all. And it was a *good* cold, the kind of cold that made you take deep breaths and think about the hot chocolate you'd have when you got home. The cool wind was a refreshing change from the sweltering summer heat that had preceded it.

The snow was in no great hurry to reach the ground. When it finally arrived it coated immobile cars and gave white highlights to the brilliant green trees and grass. Lisa was used to seeing snow on brown trees and wilted grass, not un-mowed lawns that still strained to the sky. The sight made her happy.

It was one in the afternoon, but the grey sky cast the city in a calming half-light. The day was quiet. Other than the faint noise of a distant car splashing through the small puddles forming on the roads, Lisa could hear nothing but the falling snow.

She stepped into the alley. The snow wasn't sticking here, leaving the rocks and gravel slick. They made a satisfying crunch under her sandals as she walked. She didn't see a single soul. She looked through open windows into empty kitchens and living rooms. Cars sat cold in parking spots, doors were closed and yards were empty. It was as though the summer storm had driven everyone to the warmth of their beds and the glow of their televisions, leaving Lisa with her own private day.

Snow sat in little peaks on the tops of the green picket fences and in little valleys of the loops of the chain link she passed. She left the alley, crossed a street populated only by more silent cars, and entered another back road. She passed under humming power lines occupied by solitary magpies that cawed into the void of the day.

She walked by shivering rabbits whose brown fur stood out sharply against the snow. They perked up their ears and followed Lisa with their eyes at her approach, but didn't bother moving from the divots they had dug. A little girl didn't look like much of a threat to creatures more concerned with the sudden need to stay warm.

"Hello, Howard," said Lisa.

Howard, a local rabbit who spent a lot of time nibbling on her mother's garden, wiggled his nose. Lisa didn't blame her mother for shooing Howard away, but Lisa always lured him back with an offering of lettuce and sweet peas. Lisa liked Howard, liked the way his one lopsided ear always flopped over and how he was less skittish than the other bunnies. Lisa could get within a couple steps before he bolted, and sometimes he would snatch food from her offering hand before hopping away. She liked the other rabbits too, but Howard was the only one she could identify thanks to a chunk of flesh missing from his non-lopsided ear.

"What do you think of the weather today?"

Howard blinked and hopped away.

"Well, you're rude this afternoon. Haven't I told you it's impolite to leave in the middle of a conversation?"

Howard only took a couple hops down the alley before he looked back at Lisa with soft eyes.

"What? Where are you going?"

The brown of his eyes was dreamlike through the falling snow and the grey of the alley's stones. She decided to follow Howard. Not that she believed he was trying to lead him somewhere, or even that he would end up going anywhere interesting at all. It was just the sort of day where you followed rabbits.

Howard led her further down the alley, pausing every few paces to see if Lisa was still behind him. He squirmed under a gap in a chain link fence and entered a backyard, took shelter under a tree branch that drooped low from the weight of the snow that covered it, and closed his eyes. Lisa put her fingers through the links, winced and pulled them away, and put them back after slipping on the leather gloves left in her coat pockets from last winter. She was entranced by the tranquil scene, and she watched for quite some time as the branch grew heavier and heavier. It dropped down and down and down before finally brushing the head of the sleeping rabbit.

Howard woke and lifted his head, causing the entire branch to dump its weight on him.

Lisa laughed. Howard now had a coat to match the weather, at least until he shook himself clean and bounded off in annoyance. He vanished between the thick pines that made up the border between the house and the neighbouring park, in search of a better shelter.

She wasn't sure if she should follow. The world *felt* empty, but she suspected the one moment someone else would show up was when she was trespassing through their backyard. But she was curious where Howard had gone, and she was curious what the park looked like in the soft snow. Besides, the house seemed empty, and she had vague memories of its occupants once coming over to their house for a summer barbeque and being nice enough.

She climbed over the fence while ignoring the part of her brain that felt she was purposely misremembering which house this was. She was a good climber, but even the quietest rattle of metal lingered in the day's stillness. She dropped to the ground and ducked into the trees, leaving only a few tiny footprints that would soon vanish beneath the snow that still fell.

The gap between the trees was tight, and it didn't take her into the park like she assumed. Instead she found herself in a sprawling maze of tree trunks. The branches started just high enough that she could walk without having to stoop. Snow swirled around even though needles blocked the sky. If anything, it was coming down harder. It was like she had stepped into a snow globe.

"Well if you think it's a problem, *you* tell him."

"I'm not going to be held responsible for your incompetence!"

Two children were speaking. Their voices would be beautiful if they weren't arguing.

"Hello?" Perhaps announcing herself to angry strangers wasn't the best idea, but Lisa felt rude for trespassing.

The voices cut off and were replaced with fierce whispering Lisa couldn't understand.

"Who's there?" one asked.

"Shut up!" said the other.

"You shut up!"

Silence again.

"Um, my name's Lisa. I didn't mean to interrupt, I'm just trying to find the park. I'll go try another way."

"Okay, she's leaving." Lisa thought the children were trying to be subtle, but they weren't succeeding.

"What? We can't let her go!"

"Why not?"

"What if she tells someone?"

"Tells someone what?"

"About what she saw!"

"She hasn't seen us!"

"How do you know?"

"Shoot. I guess there's only one way to know."

"What's that?"

"Hi!"

A child bounded into view. His white hair and golden eyes complimented the simple white tunic that was apparently keeping him comfortable despite the chill.

"What are you *doing*?"

"Now I know she's seen us!" the boy said to whoever was behind him.

"You idiot! Now she definitely can't leave!"

"Oh, right. Uh, hey, you! Don't move!" He tried to sound threatening, but looked friendly.

"Uh." Lisa didn't know what else to say.

"Oh, great. First you got us in this mess, and now you're just letting kids stroll in." The other child emerged, a girl identical to the boy save for longer hair and a slimmer figure.

"My name's Lisa. And you're kids, too."

The girl laughed, a light, twinkling sound. "Oh, sweetie, you have no idea."

"Ignore my partner, she's in a bad mood."

"I'm in a bad mood because *you* screwed up!"

"What's the matter?" Lisa interrupted before they could start arguing again.

"You wouldn't understand, kid."

"Maybe we should show her."

The girl stared at the boy. "Are you serious?"

"Yeah. Maybe she'll have an idea."

"You've got to be… fine, whatever. It's not like we can get much more off-schedule."

The boy brought Lisa deeper into the trees. The snow grew thicker, turning from little points of white into great, fluffy flakes.

"Here we are!" he said.

"Where's here? I can barely see." The snow clung to Lisa's eyelashes, turning the boy into a blur.

"Look on the ground."

Lisa looked down and gasped. A pure white bird was hoping in a circle. No bigger than a pigeon, the bird had broken a wing. The other flapped with every hop, and from it burst white, fluffy snow.

"What is it?"

"A snowbird." The boy said it like it was the most obvious thing in the world.

"Is it… making snow?"

"Duh. Why do you think it's called a snowbird?"

"I thought snow came from frozen water. That's what I learned in school."

"Oh, you can get snow that way too. But when the boss wants snow and the weather's not cooperating, he sends out snowbirds. This little guy's hurt, so he can't control himself."

"And whose fault is *that?*" The girl had joined them.

"I may have dropped him," the boy said with a sheepish grin.

"You may have dropped him down an *open manhole!*"

"It was an accident! Besides, he's a *bird.* Not my fault he didn't start flying."

The bird cawed in indignation. Frozen breath streamed from its beak, dropping the temperature. Lisa shivered.

"Come on, let's give him some space." The girl took Lisa's arm and led her back to where the air was warmer and the snow was thinner.

"I don't understand," said Lisa. "How come I've never seen one before?"

The girl sighed the sigh of someone who hates explaining their job. "We don't let them fly unless they're making snow. Otherwise your scientists would be all, 'Hey, what's that? We've never seen *that* kind of bird before!' and we'd be in a heap of trouble. And then when it is snowing, who's going to look up into the middle of a storm to see if there's a little bird in the middle of it?"

"So we're busy moving birds up north to get ready for winter, but then we… I messed up," says the boy, in a much more patient voice. "Now our boss is going to be annoyed because we've created a storm we weren't supposed to, and you guys are annoyed because it's all cold out when it should still be summer."

"*And* some human kid found us! Do you know what rule number one in our job is? I'll give you a hint—it's the *exact opposite of that.*"

"I'm not going to tell anyone. Who would even believe me? Besides, I think it's beautiful." The boy smiled at her, relieved to hear it.

"Well I'm glad you're enjoying this metrological disaster, but it's not all about you. The real problem is poachers," said the girl.

"Poachers?"

"Snowbirds are considered a delicacy by some… unsavoury characters," said the boy.

"He means *monsters.* Every monster around's going to be on our butts."

"And we can't call our boss for help, because we'd be in so much trouble for screwing up."

"*You'd* be in so much trouble. I'd be fine. Boss knows I'm the competent one."

"Oh yeah? Then how come you haven't gone and asked?"

"Because shut up, that's why."

"Aw, you care about me." The boy grinned at her.

"Oh, get over yourself. If you get fired, no one else will ever put up with you. Then all I'd hear is 'I need help! Please get me a job!' until my ears bleed."

"Who's your boss?" asked Lisa.

"Can't tell you. Confidentiality agreement. But if you ever get bored enough to research weather gods, I bet you'd come across him. Or her."

"Well, maybe I can help."

"You?" The girl laughed. "Thanks for the offer, kid, but I think you're a little out of your league."

"One time me and my dad saved an injured sparrow."

"Yeah? And how would your dad feel about a bird that turns his house into Antarctica?"

"I won't tell him. He can hide in my room."

"You know, that might work," said the boy. "Snowbirds heal fast, he'd only need a few days. And monsters wouldn't be able to track him because the snow would be trapped in a room."

"I can't believe you're seriously considering this. And you, kid—"

"It's *Lisa*."

"Are you sure you want to turn your bedroom into a winter wonderland? It won't be whimsical and pretty. It will be *cold*. You'll have to bundle up in a dozen blankets before you *might* fall asleep. How can we trust you to handle that? How do we know you won't give up after a day and turn that poor bird loose to get devoured?"

Lisa stared into the girl's fiery gold eyes. "You don't. But you don't want to call your boss, and it sounds like you don't want to mess with whatever these monsters are. So I can leave and you can go back to that productive discussion you were having, or you can trust a kid who thinks this is the nicest day she's ever seen."

Lisa and the girl stood off while the boy watched nervously. When the girl finally opened her mouth she was interrupted by a crash.

"They're here! No choice now!" said the boy.

"Grab the bird, kid. Fast. We can hold them off, but not for long."

Lisa ran back into the heart of the storm as roars, shouts, bangs and flashes fired off behind her. She found the bird and tried to scoop it up, but even with gloves its feathers turned her hands to ice. The creature slipped through her suddenly clumsy fingers and hit the ground with an annoyed squeak.

"Sorry!" Lisa removed her coat, turned it into a bindle, dropped the bird in it and tied the sleeves together to make a handle. The bird nestled into a ball and cooed in contentment as snow poured from the jacket.

"I got it!" Lisa shouted as she rejoined the pair. The words came through shivering teeth. With her jacket off and snow blowing straight into her body, she was now very cold.

The girl closed her eyes and put her hand on Lisa's head. A sudden warmth washed over Lisa, who now barely noticed the snow.

"That'll keep you warm until we get to your house. Which is…?"

"Just a couple blocks. Won't take long if we run. Where's the monster?"

"We drove it off. But it'll be back with friends. Come on."

The girl led them to the opening in the trees Lisa had come through. The tiny gap had been split open, with massive chunks of wood ripped away. The fence she had climbed over had been flattened.

"What kind of monsters are we dealing with, exactly?"

"The kind you shouldn't ask questions about. Just keep moving."

The snow was now coming down from the sky as heavily as it came from the bird. The wet, heavy flakes were perfect for sticking into snowballs. The boy said it was a side effect of the bird's agitation. Lisa had no idea how intelligent it was, but it seemed well aware it was being hunted.

The world was still empty. No people, no animals, no noise but their pounding footsteps. The sandals that had been so appropriate to start the day with were now tripping Lisa up. They crossed the deserted street. Lisa could hear cars in the distance, and pictured drivers waiting to get back to warm homes. She sympathised. Even with whatever the girl had done to her, the constant blowing of snow into her face was unpleasant.

She soon had a bigger problem, as six large dogs leapt over a fence and blocked the alley. No, not six—there were three, but each had two heads. Their flaming red eyes, the steam that poured from their panting mouths and the fact that they had rocky spikes instead of fur suggested that these were not animals from a local pet store.

"Stay back. Let us handle this," said the boy. The girl was already waving her hands over a snow drift that had built up against a garage. The snow rose and clumped into three balls, while a pair of branches broke off a nearby tree and flew into the side of the middle section. A huge third branch flew into the snowman's hand just in time for it to smack away a charging dog.

"Wow. How can I make my snowmen do that?"

"It takes a lot practice!" The boy had also assembled one, and was working on a second when a roar from a dog melted the first. Both heads turned its attention to the boy, and then one turned to

Lisa after her snowball nailed it in the snout. Unsure of who to attack, the two heads squabbled and nipped at each other until a smack from the new snowman sent it yipping away.

"Nice throw!"

"Thanks! It takes a lot of prac—"

Lisa got the air knocked out of her. The third dog had snuck around in the chaos and tackled her. The alley rocks cut her face, and her jacket slipped from her hands.

The dog was heavier than it looked, and it looked heavy. Its paws kept her pinned to the ground while one head rooted through her jacket. The other bared its fangs at Lisa. Its snorting breath singed her skin. Lisa winced and tried to fight back, but it was too strong. The mouth opened its slobbering jaws…

…and careened to the side as something small and brown slammed into it with tremendous force. It was Howard.

Distracted by the blur of the rabbit, the monster lost interest in Lisa and gave into its desire to chase. In a flash, both the rabbit and dog hopped a fence and vanished. The other two beasts had already slunk off, and suddenly the alley was as calm as it was when Lisa had stepped into it hours earlier. Except a fence had collapsed, another was singed, nearby tree branches were torn to shreds and a pair of hulking snowmen stood guard. But otherwise.

"I figured you'd run away the moment you saw those," said the girl as she offered Lisa a hand up. "I guess you're tougher than I thought."

"So do you trust me now?"

"Let's get you both inside before they come back."

Lisa thought she closed the back door quietly, but her mother loomed over her before she had even slipped her sandals off.

"Where were you all afternoon? And who are your friends? And *why are you bleeding?*"

"I was at the park, they're friends from school and we were playing and I just had a little accident and it's nothing! We're going to work on a school project now, please don't bother us!" Lisa threw the best lie she could think of on zero notice behind her as she ran past her mother and up the stairs to her bedroom. Her new acquaintances were right behind her.

The pair explained how to care for the snowbird, and offered a few tips on hiding him and staying warm. "We'll come collect him in a few days. And thank you," said the boy. "You have no idea how much you're helping us."

"No problem. This was fun." Lisa looked around her room with a huge grin. Snow was falling from the ceiling, but it wasn't sticking to her furniture. The snowbird, dozing in the makeshift nest they had built from torn up school notebooks and an empty shoebox, was calm now.

"You almost died," the girl said.

"Well, otherwise it was fun. Although I guess I owe a favour now." Lisa looked out the window. Howard, sporting a fresh scar on his lopsided ear, was nibbling on her mother's strawberries. The grey clouds had made way for the sun, and the summer snow glistened as it began to melt.

The pair left her bedroom and crept down the stairs, although Lisa heard the girl say, "Thanks for letting us come over, it was nice to meet you and we got a lot of homework done!" followed by a slamming door before her mother could muster a reply.

"Well, Sunny," Lisa said to the bird. "Do you mind if I call you Sunny? I'm going to call you Sunny. I'll get you some ice water and get me some hot chocolate. I don't want to find any snow in my bed when I get back, okay?"

The snowbird squawked.

The Zzzombie Apocalypse

Sure, I remember the Zombie Apocalypse. And the first thing I can tell you is that "Apocalypse" is being pretty damn generous. "Inconvenience" would be more accurate, but that doesn't glue eyeballs to TV specials. If that was an apocalypse, the fender-bender down the street last week was Carmageddon.

Here's what went down as I remember it, not as it's been sold to your generation. The parts about a top-secret research facility hidden downtown are mostly true, although I doubt every single scientist was as young, hot and promiscuous as the dramas show them. But yeah, they were playing God, or at least overly demanding Mom and Dad. Something got loose, and suddenly a bunch of people had a hankering for brains. I won't bore you with all the tedious details, so let's just say a safety inspector missed a few boxes and the next list he was ticking off was at the unemployment office.

But to claim they started terrorising the population is like claiming a mosquito you swat was terrorising your home. People called me a hero for escaping, but do you know how I got out? I *walked*. Yeah, the undead aren't exactly champion athletes. Oh sure, at first it was terrifying to see a bunch of fetid, moaning corpses shambling towards me, but once the shock wore off it was like having your fight or flight instinct kicked in by a packs of toddlers. Either option was a guaranteed victory.

I just wandered to the edge of town, where the National Guard already had a cordon up. On my way out I saw some things that, how can I put this… don't exactly jive with the narrative you've been fed. I can't say I saw any overwhelmed cops going out in blazes of glory or ordinary people heroically sacrificing themselves to save their loved ones, but I did see a SWAT team kill dozens of zombies without breaking a sweat while some old dude in a suit took it upon himself to help by knocking a bunch over with his briefcase. I hate to break it to you, but "mindless, slow moving monstrosities with no weapons but their own teeth" versus "trained professionals with guns and bite proof Kevlar" is not the knockdown drag-out battle of the century you've been taught. I saw one get curb-stomped by a child.

The whole thing was basically over by the end of the work day. Oh sure, they kept us under observation for a while, and it took some time to find the zombies that got stuck at the bottom of stairwells and crap like that. But the talking heads were struggling to come up with new stories, and the soldiers considered it a respite from serving where the enemy shoots back. Honestly, the biggest hassle was cleaning up all the blood and guts.

But pop culture nerds worldwide had fantasised about the zombie apocalypse for decades, and they just couldn't accept that it had come and gone and been so terribly, terribly lame. It started slow, survivors looking for their fifteen minutes of fame claiming they made dramatic, last-minute getaways instead of powerwalking into the sunset. Details were embellished to friends over beers, exaggerations were made to impress Twitter followers, and before you knew it we had collectively decided on an alternate timeline that was much more interesting than the mild inconvenience it had actually been.

But the truth doesn't put butts in movie seats or discs in game consoles, and it sure doesn't sell ridiculous, overpriced Zombie Survival Kits featuring whatever the hell "anti-Zombie spray" is either. A multi-billion dollar industry appeared out of thin air all because some yahoo in a lab wanted to duck out to lunch early. Look, kid, you can believe what you want. All I'm saying is that your money would probably be better spent on health insurance and beer. And stop carrying that dumb hatchet around. You look like Paul Bunyan's asshole cousin.

A Night on the Town

"Remind me why we're going to this place."

"Because we're cool, rebellious teenagers, and this is what cool, rebellious teenagers do."

"That explains you and Cheryl. Now remind me why *I'm* going. I'm neither of those things."

"You will be soon! Imagine going to school on Monday and having someone ask you, 'Hey, Alex, did you do anything interesting this weekend?' For the first time in your life you'll be able to say yes!"

"Very funny."

"Hey, don't be like that. I did you a favour, inviting you out."

"Really."

"Absolutely! I'm concerned about your low social standing, and a wild night at the hottest club in town is just what you need to get boosted up the ranks. You'll be popular in no time thanks to me."

"Uh-huh. And the fact that I'm the only person you know who could fake our chips is just a happy coincidence?"

"Yeah, life's full of wonderful surprises and crap like that. Hey look, we're here! Let's get inside, I'm freezing."

Alex sighed and watched Monica run through the drizzling rain. Then she turned her eyes up, way up, and at the peak of the skyscraper saw a blue neon sign flash "Input" to the world. The word was hazy in the mist. She looked even higher, but couldn't see the night sky through the clouds.

She entered the building. The lobby was black, save for the flicker of a few monitors, soft red mood lights and one man's bright green hair. Monica was leaning on the wall next to the security scanner, trying to look nonchalant and not doing a very good job.

When Alex joined her Monica whispered, "Okay, time to see if your skills are as good as you claim."

"Yup."

The two girls stared at each other in nervous silence. Then Monica said, "Well, after you."

"Oh no, you first. Please, I insist."

"What? No, you're going first. I'm not going to be the one getting in trouble if your hacking skills aren't what they're cracked up to be."

"Hey, you're the one who wanted to come to this stupid club. I'd be just as happy to turn around and leave."

"Alright, let's go then. Don't worry, I won't tell anyone you wimped out because you were afraid you weren't smart enough." Monica stepped towards the exit.

"Goddammit. Fine, I'll go first. But for the record, I hate you."

Monica turned back and smiled. "Now Alex, that's no way to talk to a friend. It's not my fault you're so easily manipulated."

"Ugh. At least if I get caught I won't have to spend any more time with you." Alex sighed again, then entered the scanner. She wondered if it would take note of her racing heart.

A miniature light show began. A holographic hand signaled her to stop while beams of light washed over her. Most searched her for weapons, drugs and other contraband, but it was the laser scanning her wrist that made her nervous. It was checking her ID chip, to see if she old enough to enter.

The scan dragged on, but just as Alex began to freak out the hand waved her forward. She blinked as she exited the scanner, blinded by the probing lights. The armed guard manning the machine gave Alex a long stare. She worried that after all the effort she put into outsmarting technology she was going to be caught the old-fashioned way, but the man pointed her towards the elevator. She let out a little gasp of relief.

Monica joined her a moment later. She grinned and said, "God, I can't believe that worked. I mean, nice job! I believed in you all along!"

Alex scowled. "Spare me your patronising. Scanners in clubs are easy to fool, because they use the cheap ones. They don't care if teens sneak in as long as it *looks* like they're trying to keep them out. Our money's good no matter how old we are."

"Oh. Well, I'm still impressed. I mean, they're only easy to fool by the standards of huge nerds like you, right?"

"Uh, I guess you could put it that way."

"So job well done then! Congrats, being a total loser has finally paid off for you."

"Gee, thanks. Come on, let's go before that guy gets suspicious." The guard was scrutinising Monica. Alex grabbed her arm and dragged her into the elevator.

They were joined by the neon green haired man and an elaborately tattooed woman. Alex gawked, but blushed when the woman returned the stare. She tried to look away, but was mesmerised by what she saw. The woman's eyes were artificial.

Alex recognised the model. They were new, chic, and worth more than her life savings. Designed to look like ocean water, the blue irises swirled and swayed, then splashed about as the elevator shot skyward. The woman winked at Alex, making her eyes shimmer. They reminded Alex of videos she had seen of the sun illuminating the sea.

She was brought back to reality by Monica's angry whisper. "Hey, I just checked my bank balance! I thought you said you were going to put fake info on our chips too! That cover charge was ridiculous."

"I didn't say that, you just said I should. *I* said there was no way in hell, because it's incredibly difficult to fake financial information and even if I could pull it off I'd feel guilty about robbing a place I was already sneaking into. Remember?"

"Oh yeah. Sorry, it was just a shock. Man, this place better be worth it, because I can't afford to go out again anytime soon."

The green haired man, distracted by their whispers, glanced over and sneered. "Aren't you two a little young for Input?"

"Aren't you a little old to be sticking your head in a vat of goo?" said Monica. "You look like a glow stick. An *ugly* glow stick."

The ocean-eyed woman laughed, but her companion was livid. "Listen, you little—"

The elevator door opened and the rest of his words were lost, drowned by a pulsing bassline. Alex could feel the music vibrate through her body, could feel it overload her senses. Could feel nothing else.

The club was a frenzy of people and sounds and colour. Alex gaped at the endless flashing lights, the endless mass of humanity. Everything was a blur, a senseless mess of vague shapes and glistening neon. Monica grabbed Alex's hand and pulled her into the throng. She followed, docile, her mind overwhelmed by the chaos.

They brushed past dozens of people. Alex only caught glimpses, but under the pulsating neon they looked surreal, semi-human. Most had tattoos or piercings, or more elaborate modifications—hologram projectors in their wrists, strobe lights under their skin, veins that shone like a kaleidoscope. Alex had seen all of these mods before, but in the cramped club's electric atmosphere their effects were eerie, intimidating. She was glad when Monica led her to a table in a dark and relatively quiet corner.

Monica shouted something about getting drinks and vanished. Alex sat back and surveyed the club, glad to have a moment to get her bearings. She tried to suppress her nerves and project an aura of belonging. She didn't think she succeeded.

Their table overlooked a dance floor. Alex peered over the railing, saw a teeming crowd below her. Shaking and swaying to the rapid beat, their dance was as unruly as the rest of the club. She spotted the green haired man in the corner, rubbing up against a woman. Not the one he had arrived with. Alex looked for her, and her eyes, but couldn't find her.

"Hey, look who I found!" Monica had returned, with drinks in hand and Cheryl in tow.

"What's up, Alex?" Cheryl plunked her own drink on the table and sat down. "Nice job getting us in, I knew you could do it."

"Thanks. I'm glad *someone* had faith." Alex glared at Monica, then at the drink placed before her. "What's that?"

"Apple juice." Monica rolled her eyes and took her own seat. "It's alcohol, stupid."

"Uh, could you be more specific?" Alex examined the liquid. It had been blue a moment ago, but had since turned bright green.

"Nope. Some chick at the bar was drinking one and it looked cool, so I asked for a couple. They were pretty expensive, so you can consider yours payback for getting us in."

"Great. Remind me to never do it again." Alex picked up her drink, which was now dark red. "I'm not sure I like the idea of drinking something so... shifty."

"Come on, Alex, lighten up!" said Cheryl, who took a sip of her own, unchanging, beverage. "You need to learn to unwind a little. It would do you good."

"Yeah, don't be a wimp," added Monica, who had already guzzled half of her drink. "Besides, it tastes great."

Alex put the glass to her lips and took a deep breath. She swallowed a tiny sip of the orange liquid which, to the delight of her friends, made her gag and cough.

"Well, alcohol's an acquired taste," said Cheryl, in-between giggles. "You'll get used to it."

"I can't wait."

"I'll make sure you don't!" said Monica. "I want to see some empty glasses by the end of the night!"

"I figured you'd make enough for both of us."

Cheryl laughed and turned the conversation to other matters. As she and Monica debated the pros and cons of the various nose mods that had recently become affordable to the average teen, Alex continued to look around. Something in the opposite corner caught her eye, a holographic woman moving with the music and chatting with a young man.

"Hey, what's that?" Alex pointed.

"Oh, nice!" said Cheryl. "That's one of those new Rez holograms! I didn't know they had been released here already."

"Rez?"

"Oh, she's only the most up-and-coming singer in the world," said Monica, rolling her eyes again. "She's super cool, so it's no surprise *you* haven't heard of her."

"Those holograms are supposed to be *incredibly* accurate simulations," said Cheryl. "Talking to one is like talking to Rez in person!"

"Too bad the only people who talk to holograms are losers scared of real girls," said Monica.

"Aw, come on. Plenty of normal people use them too. It's the closest we'll ever get to talking with Rez herself! They're totally different from those creepy sex-chat holograms only the real pervs use."

"Speaking of real pervs, isn't that Jordan Reeve from math? He's not making much of a case for your 'normal people do it too' argument."

"Oh wow, it is Jordan. God, I wonder what a weirdo like him talks about with a hologram."

"Only one way to find out!" said Monica. She stood. "Come on, I see an open table right next to them."

Alex shook her head, but relocated with her friends.

"I just don't know whether she likes me or not. How can you tell with girls, Rez?"

"There are always signs, Jordan." The hologram swayed to the music, but kept its eyes on the boy. "You just have to learn to interpret them."

"What do you mean?"

"Well, not all girls are as open about their feelings as I am, Jordan. You have to learn to pick up on the subtleties. Pay close attention, and you'll get answers soon enough."

"I guess. It's just so frustrating. I wish more girls were like you, Rez."

"That's very sweet, Jordan. But—" The rest of the hologram's response was drowned out by laughter from Monica and Cheryl.

Jordan turned and scowled. "I'll have to come back another time, Rez. When we can talk in *private*."

"See you later, Jordan. I hope you visit me again soon!" The hologram waved as Jordan stormed off.

"Come on, let's try it out!" said Cheryl, once the laughter had subsided.

Alex approached it. "Hi, Rez. I'm Jordan Reeve."

"Did you really think a program as sophisticated as me would fall for that?" The hologram paused to size up Alex and her friends, then returned to its dancing.

"It was worth a try. Um, I'm Alex, and this is Monica and Cheryl."

"Hello, girls. What brings you here tonight?" Even up close, the hologram's voice sounded human.

"We're just looking to have a little fun," said Monica. "Which means we don't have time to talk to—"

Cheryl cut her off. "Okay, I know you're just a computer program, but I have to tell you that I am *such* a huge fan. You're just… you're amazing."

The hologram smiled. "That's very kind of you. Are you coming to my concert next month?"

"Of course! My seat sucks, but it's still going to be awesome!"

"That's great. I'm really looking forward to that show. I think it will be a lot of fun!"

"Hey, can you give the real Rez a message for me?"

"Sure. Rez listens to all her fans' messages. Although I can't promise you'll get a response."

"Cool. Okay, tell her that—"

"Tell her that she's wonderful and whatever," said Monica. "Come on, let's hit the dance floor. I don't want to spend all night talking to a computer."

"Oh, alright. God, you're so impatient," said Cheryl. "You coming, Alex?"

"In a minute. I want to try something first."

Monica groaned. "It figures. Even at the hottest club in the city you can't tear yourself away from a computer. Fine, but if you're not on the dance floor in ten minutes I'm dragging you there myself."

"Your friend seems… forceful," said the hologram. It watched Monica and Cheryl vanish into the crowd.

"That's a polite way of putting it. So, what's it like to exist for the sole purpose of amusing drunks?"

"It's alright. I get to meet a lot of interesting people. Like you, Alex."

"Me? What's interesting about me?"

"Well, for starters, you look a little young to be clubbing."

"I don't know what you're talking about, Rez." Alex glanced around, half-expecting security to leap from the shadows.

"Oh, please. Your hacking skills may have gotten you through the door, but you're no match for my talents."

"Wait, what? How did you know I hacked our chips? You're just a hologram."

"Oh, I didn't know. But I appreciate you telling me. Ooh, I love this song!" The music had changed to a more upbeat number, and the hologram's moves shifted accordingly.

"Shit. Well played, Rez."

"Thank you. Although I must say that such language is unbecoming for a girl of your age."

"Look, if you're going to get me thrown out, make it quick and painless. Getting outsmarted by a simulation of some airhead pop star is humiliating enough."

"You're upset, so I'll overlook that insult. And you can relax. I'm not throwing you out."

"You're not?"

"Nope. Well, not as long as you do me a favour."

"A favour? What kind of favour could a dancing computer program want?"

"I do more than just dance, you know."

"Yes, I can see you're also skilled at dragging out conversations."

The hologram laughed. It was a strange, crystalline noise. Unlike its speaking voice, it sounded fake. Too perfect to be human.

"I need you to go down to the dance floor and find a couple people." The hologram held out its hands, and two figures flashed into existence above them. They were the green haired man and the ocean-eyed woman, in miniature.

"Uh, okay. Can do." Alex turned to leave.

"Hold on, kid, there's more. Once you've found them you need to, discreetly and casually, ask to buy some accel."

"What?" It took Alex a moment to process the hologram's request. "You want me to buy drugs? What the hell for?"

"I think they'll help you relax. You seem stressed."

"Rez, you're testing my patience."

"What, can't a girl have a little fun? Oh, all right. Look, they've been selling accel here for a few weeks now."

"Okay, so what? It's illegal. Just tell security and they'll turn them in to the cops. Problem solved."

"It's not that simple. Input turns a blind eye to their little business in exchange for a cut. It's worth the risk given the amount of money involved. But that might change if they were caught doing something unsavoury."

"Like selling an addictive psychotropic to an underage girl."

The hologram grinned. "You catch on fast."

"I still don't see what's in this for you. You're a hologram, what do you care about drug dealers?"

"Do a good job and maybe I'll tell you." The hologram laughed again.

Alex groaned. "Wait, hang on. Isn't this going to end with the club learning I'm underage anyway? I get screwed no matter what."

"If you do as I say I promise nobody will find out. It will be our dirty little secret." The hologram winked.

"Great. Just great. You know, Rez, this may shock you, but I've never bought drugs before. What exactly am I supposed to say?"

"Whatever comes to mind. Relax, you'll be fine. Dealers are always on the lookout for nervous kids who want to experiment. You're their perfect customer."

"Well, I guess I don't have a choice. But I better get free concert tickets out of this."

Another laugh. "Nothing's free here, kid. Speaking of which, hit an ATM first. I think we still have one somewhere."

Alex walked away and was soon absorbed by the crowd. Once out of the hologram's sight she ran straight for the elevator. She knew fleeing would probably get Monica and Cheryl in trouble, but at that moment she found it hard to care.

Her escape attempt was short-lived. As Alex waited for the elevator, a nearby monitor flashed a message. "Leaving so soon? Well, say hi to the guard on the way out for me! – R"

Alex stomped her foot and swore. She hadn't expected to escape, but it was still infuriating to be outwitted by a computer program. For a moment she stood and stared at the elevator, fantasising about blitzing past the guard and dashing into the night. Then she searched for stairs down to the dance floor.

***

The dance floor was even more chaotic than the rest of the club. Tightly packed figures, flickering in and out of neon spotlights, gyrated to booming bass. Alex could barely hear herself think.

"It's about time!" Monica emerged from the crowd and grabbed Alex's arm. She was swaying, but not in time to the music.

"Yeah, I just couldn't resist. Where's Cheryl?"

"Last I saw she was grinding with some cute boy. Hey, you should find yourself a guy too." Monica giggled.

"Good idea. In fact, I think I see one right now." Alex saw green hair bobbing with the beat in the corner.

She pulled away from Monica and squeezed into the mob. The floor was so packed she couldn't help but rub against dozens of sweaty bodies, but they were either too focused on their dancing or too intoxicated to care. The music swelled as she moved further in. By the time she emerged on the far side it made her tremble.

The green haired man was dancing with a tall blonde. They appeared to be locked in an intimate embrace, but something about their motion was wrong. They weren't moving with the rhythm. It wasn't long before the blonde left the man's arms and wandered away. He continued to dance as if nothing had happened.

Alex approached him. When he didn't turn to look at her she cleared her throat and said, "Hey."

The man ignored her. "Hey!" she said again, louder.

No response. Alex shook his arm. "Hey!" she shouted.

The man gave her a glance, then looked away.

"Hey!" Alex shouted once more. "You want to dance?"

He gave her a withering stare. "You don't look like the dancing type."

Alex wrapped her arms around his waist and started swaying to the music. "Then you'll have to teach me."

The man hesitated, but took hold of her. They danced in silence, Alex tripping over her feet as her mind raced to think of what to say.

To her relief, her partner spoke first. "You look familiar."

"I came up on the elevator with you."

"Right. Were you the one being a prick?"

"No, that was my, uh... acquaintance."

"Well, maybe your *acquaintance* can give you some dance tips. You're terrible."

"Hey, that's not fair. I've only stepped on you once." Alex slipped as she spoke. "Okay, twice."

"Well, until you learn to put your feet where they belong, I think you should dance with someone else." The man let go of her.

"Wait!" Alex tightened her grip. "The truth is, I didn't really come here to dance."

The man hesitated again, then pulled Alex close. Very close. He held her head against his chest, leaned down to her ear and whispered, "Then what *did* you come here for?"

Alex could feel the man's heart beat through his sweat stained shirt. "I heard you were selling something… interesting."

"How much?"

"What?"

"*How much do you want?*"

"Um…"

"Alright, since you're obviously a virgin, I'll be gentle. Two hits, no more. Wouldn't want you and your friend overdosing. Well, maybe your friend."

"What's that going to cost me?"

The man didn't answer until a pair of other dancers drifted past. "Thirty bucks a hit. Cash. And for God's sake, start acting like you belong here."

"I *don't* belong here," muttered Alex.

"What?"

"I said, how do I pay you without looking suspicious?"

"Follow my lead." The man wrapped his arms around Alex's neck, and she reciprocated. He glanced around the room as they danced and then, without warning, kissed her.

She wanted to pull away, but the man held her tight. After a few moments he withdrew and said, "Slip it in my back pocket," before returning to her lips.

Alex shoved one hand into her jeans and fumbled for some bills. She pulled the cash out and put her hand on the man's back. He grabbed her arm and guided her further down. Alex jammed the money in his pocket and got her mouth free.

"Do you always make your customers grope your ass?"

"A girl touching my ass looks less suspicious than a girl slipping me money. Keep dancing with me for a minute, then find my partner. She'll get you your merchandise."

"It's a two-part process?"

"You think we're stupid enough to keep our profits and goods in the same place? Now shut up and dance."

Alex stepped back into the crowd a minute later. She wandered, unsure of where to find the ocean-eyed woman. Then she felt a hand on her arm.

"Wanna dance?" The woman's eyes splashed in time to the song's thumping beat.

"Sure." Alex let the woman grab her waist and pull her close as the music changed to a slow pulse.

The woman rested her head on Alex's shoulder. "I hope my associate didn't give you too much trouble."

"Not really." Alex could feel the warmth of her body, could smell her lavender perfume. "So, are you going to give me my… purchase?"

With one smooth motion, the woman produced a tiny plastic bag and slipped it in Alex's front pocket. It was an act she must have performed hundreds of times, in dozens of dark clubs throughout the city. She let her hand linger, just for a moment.

"Thanks."

"We could still dance, if you'd like." The woman lifted her head and stared at Alex. Her eyes were calm now.

"Don't you have other, um, customers?"

"Yeah. But sometimes it's nice. To just dance." She lowered her head again.

Alex hesitated, then put her arms around the woman. She let her nose brush her lavender hair.

"How can you make a living like this?"

She was lit up by a neon red spotlight, then plunged back into darkness. "I used to ask myself that. Now it's all I *can* do. There's something about places like this I find… addictive. There's just so much *life* in them."

Alex looked at the couple dancing next to them. They made her uncomfortable. Their movements were mechanical, their faces grim. "I'm sorry, but I have to go. Maybe another time."

"Well, you know where to find me." The woman kissed Alex's cheek before releasing her.

Alex slipped into the crowd. She looked back once, saw the ocean-eyed woman being boxed in by the couple beside her.

She touched her cheek, then left the dance floor.

***

"Alright, I did your stupid errand," said Alex to the hologram.

"And you did a great job," said Rez. The hologram was still dancing. It would continue until it was shut down at dawn.

"So can I go now?"

"Sure. But feel free to stay and chat."

"Very funny. Hey, what do I do with the accel I bought? I can't just walk out of here with it."

"What accel?"

"Don't play games with me, you dumb light show." Alex reached into her pocket. "*This* acc—" She stopped mid-sentence. It was gone.

"You need to be careful in a place like this. Things can get stolen."

"Cute. Well, I'm out of here. So long, Rez."

"Hang on. There's something I need to tell you."

"Make it fast."

"I've given you a little payment for your services. Two hundred dollars, plus what you paid for the accel, deposited in your bank account. Just my way of saying thanks for being such a good sport."

"Oh. Um, cool. Thanks."

"Don't mention it."

"So who's footing the bill? Will you tell me now?"

"Maybe it's a government agency trying to crack down on narcotics. Or maybe a rival club is coercing dealers into working for them. Could be a supplier that isn't getting their cut. You don't need to know the details."

"Fine, be mysterious. I don't even care."

"Whatever you say. Are you leaving now?"

"As soon as I find my friends."

"Goodbye then, Alex. Come back soon! Well, as soon as you're old enough." The hologram laughed its artificial laugh.

"Yeah, I can't wait." Alex took a step away, turned back. "Rez, what will happen to those two?"

"Nothing they don't deserve. Let's leave it at that."

"Okay. Goodbye, Rez."

Alex left the hologram, which had already turned its attention to another patron. As she searched for Monica and Cheryl she passed the green haired man being dragged to the elevator by a couple who looked a little too serious to be in a club. The man struggled and shouted at Alex, but she couldn't make out his words.

The ocean-eyed woman was behind him. She didn't fight her escort, had accepted whatever her fate was. She stared at Alex as she passed by. Her eyes were motionless. Alex couldn't meet them.

***

"I can't believe you danced with that green haired creep," said Monica as they rode the elevator.

"I can't believe you danced with a girl!" said Cheryl. "You never struck me as the type."

"Didn't you two have anything better to do than spy on me?" Alex blinked and rubbed her ears, adjusting to the lack of strobe lights and loud music.

"Hey, it's not every day we see you socialising. This was a rare opportunity!" said Cheryl.

"I knew you had it in you," said Monica. "Admit it, Alex, you had fun."

"Not really. Although I did make two hundred bucks. That was nice."

"What? How?" her friends asked in unison.

"I'll tell you about it tomorrow," said Alex as the doors slid open.

Monica and Cheryl strolled through the security scanner. Alex paused before entering, and breathed deep when she was allowed to pass.

"So, same time next week?" asked Monica.

"No, thanks," said Alex. "This place just wasn't exciting enough for me, you know?"

"Funny. And just when I thought you were going to start acting like a normal person."

"Sorry to get your hopes up."

They left the building. Rain was pouring down, though Alex could barely hear it over the ringing in her ears. She looked up at the night sky, but even the club's neon sign was lost in the downpour. All that was visible was a billboard, an animated advertisement for artificial eyes that looked like the ocean. Alex sighed and started to walk home.

Storybook Endings

My Stepmother always told me to be scared of the witch in the woods. Oh, how she delighted in telling me bedtime stories about the witch turning disobedient girls into toads, or bathing in their blood, or just gobbling them right up. I spent many sleepless nights lying still, terrified the witch was lurking in the shadows. When morning came I would resolve to work twice as hard and listen to every word Stepmother said, so the witch would have no quarrel with me.

As I grew older I stopped believing in the witch, so Stepmother found other ways to motivate me. The switch, the riding crop, the simple back of her hand. If I cried, she would continue until I stopped, but then I would be too battered and bruised to finish my work, so out would come her tools again. I don't cry anymore.

Father objected, but he was a weak man. Stepmother would make him back down, and the "correction" would continue with renewed vigour. Later, after she exhausted herself, Father would come into my room and nurse my wounds. He would hug me and stroke my hair and tell me that Stepmother meant well, that we shouldn't question her. And I would nod my head and say nothing, but I would wonder what happened to the man who seemed so strong when I was a little girl.

One day I ripped the dress I was mending, Stepmother's favourite. It was an accident, but she was convinced otherwise. I won't deny I had often considered it, but the satisfaction wouldn't have been worth the punishment. She flew into a rage, and I was so upset about being blamed that I did the unthinkable. I talked back.

I called her words girls should never use, and then the switch and the crop were no longer enough. Out came the fireplace poker, all nice and warm. But Stepmother went too far, and this time Father would not back down. She shouted and threatened and used the very words I was beaten for, but Father stood his ground. So though I was watching my skin blister and crack, I couldn't help but smile. Father had finally become a prince, just like Mother had always called him, and he was going to save me.

I don't remember Mother's face, only her quiet voice. She told me bedtime stories too, but a very different kind. Tales of beautiful princesses rescued from cruel fates by handsome princes, who would return together to their kingdom to live happily ever after. When I was a little girl I dreamed of being a storybook princess, of living in a castle and ruling over my loving subjects. When Stepmother arrived, my dreams shrunk. I would have lived in bliss as a farmer's wife, so long as my husband was a prince inside.

Those dreams were beaten out of me, but they rushed back when Father at last came to my rescue. In my mind, Father would banish Stepmother, and then one day a prince would come into my life. We would fall in love and have many children, and I would be a wonderful mother.

But there was no banishment. The next day, Stepmother apologised for her awful words and deeds, and swore she would never lay another finger on me. She even offered to go deep into the woods, to gather herbs that would soothe my aching burns. I was suspicious, but Father was a forgiving man. He even volunteered to go himself, saying that Stepmother didn't need to prove herself. Father didn't believe that a witch lived in the woods. Poor Father.

Night fell, and Father had not returned. Stepmother fretted, but her words of concern rang hollow. There was something in her eyes, a glint no false speech could hide.

I woke to the bleating of a lamb. Confused, I stumbled out into the frosty morning. A black lamb nuzzled at me. It had been standing right outside our door. I bent down to pet it, and it licked my face. I giggled and hugged it tight. Feeling it shiver, I brought it in from the cold. It wouldn't stop bleating once inside. It butted at me, trying to push me back towards the door. The noise awoke Stepmother before I could decide what to do.

She took one look at the lamb and fetched her butcher's knife. I protested, arguing that the lamb must be lost and that we should return it to its shepherd. Stepmother said we were going to have to be more resourceful without Father to provide for us. She ordered me out of the way, false niceties from the day before disappearing.

The lamb hid behind me, its bleats now shrill and panicked. I tried to get it to the door, but Stepmother shoved me aside and slit its throat before my eyes. She stroked my cheek with a bloody hand and ordered me to sit and watch as she slaughtered it.

We had lamb stew for supper. I thought about refusing to eat, but I knew how that would end. And I *was* hungry. Stepmother was stingy with our stockpiles, at least when it came to my servings. She was generous that night though, dishing out bowl after bowl. In good spirits, she put aside her usual criticisms of me to discuss how delicious the lamb was. And she was right, though I wouldn't acknowledge it.

Afterwards, she insisted on telling me a bedtime story. I was leery of her desire to do what she hadn't done in years, but if it would keep her in her good mood I wouldn't argue. So she told me a story. A story about the witch in the woods, who some called the Shepard because she liked to take lost men and turn them into harmless little lambs. Then she kissed me on the forehead, smiled, and bid me sweet dreams.

I thought of my father's bushy black hair and threw up.

I didn't sleep that night. I lay still, staring at the roof, fantasising of slitting Stepmother's throat the way she slit Father's. Then I had a better idea.

I renounced my fantasies, the dream that all I had to do was sit and wait for a prince to make everything better. Real princes don't care about girls like me. And men who act like princes get killed for their trouble. In my world, good intentions don't make up for ignorance. A true princess wouldn't wait for anyone or anything. She would take what she wanted, when she wanted it. True princesses have power they don't hesitate to use.

I slipped from my bed. I dressed in traveller's clothes, strapped Father's knife to my belt, and struck out into the night. A light snow fell as I walked. The night was silent, and only the faintest rays of moonlight trickled through the clouds. I must have stood out, red cloak against snow and night. I felt the hilt of the knife and smiled.

But I hesitated at the edge of the forest. I had never been this close, let alone entered the trees. I breathed deep. *A princess is brave. A princess is strong. A princess does not hesitate.*

I shivered when I crossed into the woods, though nothing happened. After the first step the rest came easier, and soon I was deep inside. The forest is a gloomy place. Twisted roots trip you.

Branches and briars scrape at your skin. No light shines, not even in the day. There are no paths, no easy ways through. Only trees and trees and trees. I don't know how long I wandered. I had no idea where I was or where I needed to go. I just trudged on, driven by anger and sheer stubbornness.

Ravens flew from tree to tree above me, peering down in silence. At first I thought nothing of them, but there was something in the way they looked at me. They were too knowing. I followed them to a clearing. A crumbling stone house sat at the far edge. In the middle a woman in black, her back to me, worked at a cauldron. Ingredients were carefully measured, the mixture delicately stirred, the result gingerly tasted. Repeat, repeat, repeat. I stood and watched for a long time before approaching and clearing my throat.

"My name is—"

"I know your name," said the woman, her voice rasping. "Do you think you would be here if I didn't want you?"

"I..." I didn't know how to respond. She laughed.

"My ravens watched you. Do you not wonder how you found me? I control the trees. There are no paths but what I dictate."

She turned around. She had been beautiful once, when she cared about beauty. Now her face was scarred, her wild hair filthy, her teeth decayed. But she still had a certain aura about her, a passion that made me want to flee. *A princess is brave.*

"Why are you here? Most that enter my forest are lost lambs. But you have purpose."

"I want to be your apprentice."

Another laugh, long and loud. "Apprentice? What makes you think I want a little runt as an apprentice?"

"I'm not a runt. I'm strong."

The witch grunted. "Well, you were brave to come, I'll grant you that. But if you think that's enough, you'd best think again. Would you like to know how my master chose me?"

I nodded.

"I was older than you, though not by much. The most beautiful girl in town—their words, not mine. Every boy fancied me. I flirted, and read, and made clothes in my parents' shop. I was happy enough.

"Then the plague came. It swept through fast, infecting half the town before anyone knew. The royal doctors declared us beyond help and ordered a quarantine. Anyone who tried to escape was cut down by arrows. They would wait until we all died or fought through it. If you haven't heard plague stories, child, then let's just say your odds of the latter were slim.

"I and a few others beat those odds. Many who didn't took their time dying, and suddenly our greatest enemy was starvation and thirst. Our reserves were low, and the outside world wouldn't give into our pleas for more. Not until the diseased were dead and burned.

"I tried to be patient. I truly did. But did the sick have the courtesy to accept fate and die? No. They ate our food, drank our water, threatened my life so they could prolong theirs for a few miserable days. Death would have been a mercy, but they were too scared to admit that their end had come.

"So one night, with my throat aching of thirst, I slit their throats one by one. They looked at me with such shock and anger as they died, but I didn't begrudge them. I held their hands. I killed my neighbours, my friends, all the boys who had tried to kiss me and the one boy I let succeed. And when a healthy man nursing his dying wife tried to stop me, I slit his throat too.

"I left my parents for last. They were so sick they could barely speak, but with cracked lips they asked their daughter to bring them water. Did they not want their own flesh and blood to *live?* I loved my parents, but they were such *cowards.*

"Still, I hesitated. I stood outside our home for so long, wondering if I was truly the sort of person who could do it. It would be mercy for us all, but could anything justify such a terrible sin?"

The witch had been strolling towards me as she spoke, and here she paused to give me a terrible smile.

"Well, you know the answer. I killed my father first, thinking my mother would handle the surprise better. But oh, how she screamed and screamed. She made my hands shake so much that I made a terrible mess of her neck. My poor mother. It must have been painful. But I tried!

"The other survivors were horrified, but it's hard to get outraged when you're starving. They put aside their judgement long enough to help me burn the bodies. The stench was terrible, but the sweet taste of fresh water washed it away.

"And then they threw me out, betrayed me for the crime of saving them. But someone saw what I had done. Someone who had unleashed the plague in the hopes of finding a suitable apprentice. It turned out I was more than suitable."

The witch's rancid breath swept over my face, bringing tears to my eyes. My knees shook, my heart raced. I wanted to vomit. *A princess is brave.*

She brought down the hood of my cloak. She stroked my cheek. Her touch was gentle, but it made me shiver.

"So, child. Do you still want to be my apprentice?"

A princess doesn't hesitate. "Yes."

"Hmm. I hadn't intended to take an apprentice for quite some time, but you've made me curious. And if you turn out to be less brave than you act, well, I'll have other uses for you. Come, child."

"I have a name. It's—"

"It's what I wish it to be. And you will call me Master. Do you understand?"

"Yes. Master."

She led me to her cauldron, where a goopy brown potion simmered. Bones floated on its surface.

"Wait here." She went into her hovel and returned with a book, a leather bag and a much smaller cauldron.

The thick book was bound in worn black leather. The pages were yellow and ragged, and the witch flipped through them with the delicacy normally reserved for holding a newborn babe.

"Is that your spell book, Master?"

"My grimoire, yes. I took it from my master, who took it from hers, and so it's gone for longer than anyone knows. You must never touch it without my permission. It contains magic that terrifies even me."

She found the page she wanted and whispered under her breath as she studied it. Apparently satisfied, she handed me the bag.

"Open it."

A foul stench greeted me. The bag was full of plants, minerals and pieces of dead animals.

"Magic, child, is not something anyone can learn. In some, it flows like blood. In others, it is anathema. The only way to tell is to test you."

"Are you going to make me perform a spell, Master?"

"No. We are going to prepare a potion, and then you will drink it. It will be unpleasant."

"What does it do, Master?"

"It will try to kill you. Whether or not it succeeds will determine your magical nature. Whether you can translate that nature into skill is another matter entirely. But don't worry. It kills most people, so it probably won't come to that." She smirked. "Are you scared, child? I warned you. It's too late to back down."

"I'm not scared." I was terrified. *A princess is brave.*

"Then reach in there and get me a sprig of holly."

I did as I was told, handing her all sorts of ingredients both mundane and strange. When she was done, the mixture was milky white.

"Now, come here. By my side."

She plucked a hair from my head without warning and dropped it in the cauldron. I grimaced, but didn't protest.

"A hair, to test your mind. Now spit into it."

I did as told.

"Saliva, to test your body. And blood, to test your spirit. Give me your hand."

The witch took my hand in hers. It was ice cold. She took a knife from her robes and drew it across my thumb. We watched my blood drip.

"And finally my blood, to bind you to me." She sliced her own thumb, and with the first drop the mixture turned pitch black.

"Now drink it. All of it."

"Master, what happened to your master?"

"I killed her. I gave her a slow, painful death. For my parents."

"Oh." *A princess does not hesitate.*

I drew my knife and plunged it in her heart. She didn't make a sound, but I saw the shock and anger in her eyes as she fell. Her lips moved, trying to form words that would curse me and save her. I held a hand over her mouth, and in my other hand took one of hers, and I waited for the twitching to stop.

Witches can be so foolish. They cover their homes with wards to guard against magical foes, yet don't take even the slightest precaution against mundane weapons. Their arrogance is so often their downfall.

I cleaned my knife, then picked up the cauldron and drank. It tasted like ash.

I don't quite recall what happened next. It's a blur, a fuzzy stream of hallucinations and delirium, madness and rage. I was sick for days, maybe weeks. But I lived.

My Stepmother thinks me long dead. She has remarried, had two children of her own. Twins, a handsome boy and a beautiful girl, now nearly the age I was when I fled. Just like in a story she once told me. Oh, the witch had such clever uses for them in that tale.

My Stepmother is not scared of the witch in the woods. But she should be. After all, a princess always gets what she wants.

A Homeowner's Dilemma

"You want to sell? In this market?"

"I just don't think this is the house for us," said my wife. She sat across from me at the kitchen table, nursing a cup of tea.

"You could have mentioned that before we took out a twenty year mortgage."

"That was before we knew about the… problems." The kitchen table quivered at the word.

"Yeah, and before we sunk thousands of dollars into repairs. Not to mention all the time *I* spent renovating. Where was 'I just don't think this is the house for us' when I was installing those fancy European faucets you insisted on?"

"We can take the faucets with us." She sipped her tea.

"Can we take the bedroom's fresh paint with us? Can we take Jimmy's treehouse with us? Can we take the *refurbished basement I slaved away at for days with us?*"

"The basement is what caused this mess!" It rumbled, as if to prove her point.

"Don't get mad at me. How was I supposed to know it was on top of an ancient Indian burial ground?"

"If you had just been a little more careful—"

"I know, I know, I wouldn't have enraged the dead." I rolled my eyes. As if it was *my* fault. It's not like you learn how to avoid disturbing the supernatural in shop class. "If you want to blame someone, blame the real estate agent."

"Speaking of which, did you *talk* to him?"

"Yes, and—" I paused to let a bloodcurdling shriek from the attic fade. "And he said that since we already signed the contract there's nothing he can do to get us out of it."

"And you just *accepted* that?" My wife sighed and moved to the chair next to me. She wasn't trying to smooth over the argument with physical intimacy—her old chair had begun to float.

"I was going to argue, but my phone started screeching Satanic prayers so I had to hang up." I ducked as the chair zoomed over my head.

"See, that kind of inconvenience is exactly why I think we should sell!" She grabbed the chair as it made a second pass. "Do you mind?" she said to it. "We're trying to have a conversation here."

"I'd rather put up with a little inconvenience than lose a *lot* of money."

"A *little?* I don't call being woken up every night by the restless wailing of the dead to be a *little* inconvenient." She tried to wrestle the chair to the ground as she spoke.

"You'll get used to it. Remember when you couldn't sleep through my snoring?" I stood up to rearrange the letter magnets on the fridge. They were spelling "LEAVE THIS PLACE" again.

"The neighbours won't! Do you have any idea how many complaints we've got?" The chair broke free and flew into the living room.

"So? The Johnsons never mow their lawn, the Browns' dog digs up every garden on the block, and our house emits the howls of the damned. Nobody's perfect." I opened the fridge to grab an apple, but all the fruit rotted beyond recognition before my eyes. I settled for a beer.

"Oh, come on. That isn't the same and—" There was a crash from the living room. "And that better not have been my grandmother's china!"

"Or what? Am *I* the one flying around the living room?" I sat back down and opened the beer. Dozens of worms crawled out of it.

"You're the reason our furniture is possessed! Look, even if *we* can tough this out, what about the kids? Jimmy's too young to be hearing some of the language the undead use." My wife took another sip of tea, then made a face and spit it out. "Ugh, it turned into goat's blood again."

"We can't shelter Jimmy forever. He's going to have to learn what those words mean sooner or later."

"But he doesn't have to hear them from a vengeful spirit! Last night one told him it was going to 'suck the marrow from his bones' before it 'dragged him into the depths of hell.' That's awful!"

"Don't be melodramatic. I'm sure Jimmy's heard 'hell' before."

"There were other words I don't care to repeat. But more importantly, *our son was threatened!*" She got up to make a fresh cup of tea, but the water started boiling with such ferocity that she was forced away.

"Well, maybe it will toughen him up. I was bullied when I was a kid, and it helped me in the long run."

"Were you bullied by ghosts?"

"No, but—"

"And what about Susan?"

"What about her?"

As if on cue, Susan shouted down the stairs. "Mom! Dad! One of the wraiths keeps threatening to 'fill my womb with countless maggots!' I'm trying to study!"

"Well, you just tell it that *you're* in charge of what goes in your body!" To me my wife said, "a thirteen-year-old girl has enough to worry about as it is! She shouldn't have to deal with wraiths too!"

"Why not? Maybe it will give her a little perspective. Her junior high drama seems awfully trivial in comparison, right?"

"You're unbelievable." The haunting moans of a hundred dying men punctuated her sentence. The dying men moans always took her side.

"Now it's telling me 'my body is a fragile vessel that will soon decay, leaving my soul exposed to an eternity of perpetual torment!' I have an algebra test tomorrow, you know!"

Billy joined the conversation too. "Mommy, what does 'eviscerate' mean?"

"I'll be right up, you two!" My wife sighed. "Be honest with me. Is this really about the money, or are you just being stubborn?"

"You're damn right I'm being stubborn. This is *our* house, we paid good money for it, and I'm not about to abandon it just because a bunch of whiny Indians got their graves desecrated. I'm not going to be that petty when *I* die."

"Will you at least look into having an exorcism performed?" The curtains caught fire in response to the suggestion. My wife doused them.

I didn't reply until visions of our grisly deaths stopped being projected into our brains. "Forget it! We're trying to *save* money here. Have you seen how much exorcists charge? Besides, this will all blow over. They'll get bored of haunting us and go hang out in an abandoned amusement park or something."

The lights turned blood red, the stove roared with a searing heat, the sink spewed entrails and a swarm of locusts appeared out of thin air.

"BORED?" said a booming, disembodied voice that shook the entire house, "WE SHALL NEVER BORE OF TORMENTING YOU. EVERY DAY OF YOUR PUNY LIVES WILL BE FULL OF AN AGONY SO PURE YOU WILL PRAY FOR A DEATH THAT WILL NEVER BE GRANTED. FOR AS LONG AS YOU INTRUDE ON OUR SACRED LAND YOU WILL KNOW NOTHING BUT SORROW AND THE TRUE MEANING OF PAIN."

My wife said nothing. She just looked at me with her "I told you so" expression.

"Alright, alright! I'll call the agent and tell him we want to sell. Are you happy now?"

She nodded. The entrails stopped spewing, and the locusts vanished.

"I hope you understand just how much money we're going to lose."

The fridge magnets arranged themselves into a crude taunt. I stood up to scatter them, and got nailed in the back of the head by the flying chair.

Distant Memories, Distant Drones

Sometimes, when it's quiet, I can remember what my life was like before moving to Cedar Springs. I had a house, a wife (Mary? Margery?). A child, I think, or maybe just a cat. I keep trying to check the family photos in my wallet, before remembering the guards took them when I arrived. I can barely remember them now either.

I must have had a stable job, because how else could I have bought a house? I think I worked in an office, since I have a few ties and nice shirts. Maybe I was a lawyer, or an accountant. Or maybe I was just a waiter at a fancy restaurant.

I have a job here in Cedar Springs too. I'm a fisherman. I've gotten pretty good at it over the years, though the fish are scarce these days. Nobody's sure why. All we can agree on is that we're not overfishing. I don't get paid to fish—no one gets paid here—but if I didn't do my part, Cedar Springs wouldn't function. So even though I'm just a fisherman, I feel more important than I think I felt at my old job.

It's lonely in Cedar Springs, but beautiful. My old house was in a bland suburb, the kind you could find in a dozen different cities (Which did I call home?). I remember going outside every morning and seeing nothing but pavement and houses that looked much like mine, occupied by people much like me. Maybe that's why I can't remember a lot about my old life. Maybe there wasn't a lot worth remembering.

I just have a one room cabin here, but it's all I need. Now when I go outside in the morning I see snow-capped mountains and the river in the valley where I fish. I hear rushing water, wind, birdcalls. Sometimes I even hear a wolf or deer but, like the fish, they're getting rare.

Then there are the cedars, of course. A few of the needles are turning brown for the fall, but seeing the sun illuminate the rest at dawn is like seeing a field of swaying emerald. My cabin is made of cedar wood, like every building here. But no matter how many we cut down, we don't put a dent in the forest. The cedars are countless.

Climb to the highest point in town and you'll see nothing but trees for miles and miles. Sometimes it's hard to remember there's a world beyond them.

We haven't cut down all that many, now that I think about it. After all, there are only a couple hundred people here. We don't know the exact number. Nobody's bothered to count, and people used to come and go. Now they just go.

None of us knew each other before we arrived at Cedar Springs, and none of us remember why we came. There are plenty of theories: nuclear war, climate change, biological disaster, and on and on. A couple people have even suggested that aliens invaded, or that we're all part of a government experiment. I used to laugh at them, and most people still do, but as the years went by without outside contact I figured those are as good of an explanation as any.

There are also plenty of theories as to why our memories are so poor. Some think it's something the cedars are giving off, or something in the water. Others believe it's something we were exposed to before we came here. I, like most, blame the drones.

The drones buzz overhead at all hours, like we're living in a hornet nest. Usually they're hidden by the clouds, but the noise lets us know they're near. Every now and then one will come into view, a soaring grey metal bird, but we can do nothing but watch and wonder. We don't know what they want with us, if they're observing us or spraying chemicals or God knows what else. All we know is that something about the noise forces our memories from our heads. Images of my house and wife (Megan? Miranda?) slip from my mind until quiet returns to Cedar Springs.

It's quiet more often lately. When we first came the drones were a constant presence, but now they leave us alone for a morning or afternoon. A few weeks ago one crashed nearby, something we hadn't thought possible. We had begun to think of them as a natural phenomenon, or even supernatural beings. A roar of thunder and a fireball reminded us they were built by our fellow man.

Adam, the closest Cedar Springs has to a mechanic, investigated. He found the crash site, a charred pit in the woods, but the wreckage was gone. In its place was a soldier. We never learned his name, so we took to calling him the Stranger. Adam found him under a tree, unconscious. He couldn't wake him, so he carried him back to what passes for our clinic.

The guards didn't search him, because the guards had all left. They vanished into the wilderness over a few months, although we think some snuck back and claimed to be newcomers. We couldn't be sure—they had disguised themselves, and our memories were as unreliable as ever. But there was something in their eyes that made us wonder.

We searched the Stranger, but found nothing unusual. He was unarmed, so we figured he wasn't a threat. We assumed he was either helping recover the drone or trying to stop those who were, and whichever it was something went wrong. It didn't matter. What was important was that he was an outsider, with memories and knowledge.

After a couple days in the clinic Doc Johnston had him awake and talking. The Doc sounded strange when he made the announcement, like he was shell-shocked. When questioned, he just said that treatment had been difficult, that he needed a walk to clear his head. A day later we realised he wasn't coming back.

Meanwhile, the Stranger was questioned by Old Margaret (Was that my wife's name? Margaret?), who was kind of like our mayor. She hadn't been elected or anything, but she was as smart as any of us, and her age commanded respect. Cedar Springs automatically turned to her in a crisis, like a child turning to their mother.

Old Margaret and the Stranger talked for hours. We'll never know what they talked about, because the moment Old Margaret stepped out the clinic's door she announced a ban on visiting him. The Cedar Springs Police Force (a half-dozen volunteers with batons and old pistols who did little more than break up the odd fight) would guard the clinic around the clock. As soon as the Stranger was healthy enough to leave he would, and that would be that. Anyone who tried to speak with him "wouldn't like the consequences."

We had never seen Old Margaret employ force, and it scared us. Most people accepted her law, figuring she knew what was best for us. Adam, too curious for his own good, tried to force his way inside, figuring the police couldn't bring themselves to seriously harm anyone. The officer on watch beat his face to a pulp. Enraged, Adam threatened to leave Cedar Springs, taking his tools and expertise with him, unless Old Margaret granted him an audience with the Stranger. She called his bluff. Knowing that we had all long forgotten where the nearest town was, Adam backed down. That little episode dissuaded anyone who was still interested.

Me, I just went back to fishing. I tried to forget the Stranger, like I've forgotten so much else. But sitting by the river for hours at a time, away from the noise of Cedar Springs and doing nothing but waiting for a bite, my mind couldn't help but wander. When the drones left me alone I was sometimes able to dredge up more memories of the life I had left behind. I didn't dwell on them, until one day I was able to remember my wife's name (Maureen? No…), her face, her voice. Her laugh. Then I had to know everything.

I dug out my little stash of whisky and waited until Jack pulled the graveyard shift at the clinic door. Jack and I were the best of friends that two people could be in Cedar Springs. I made sure he got the plumpest fish, he made sure I got the freshest vegetables, and we both made sure we had plenty of moonshine.

It didn't take much to convince him to drink on the job. There hadn't been any trouble at the clinic since Adam's incident, and he could never say no to alcohol. I got him talking, then singing, then snoring.

The door was locked. I searched Jack for a key, but apparently Old Margaret didn't trust him with one. So I took his baton and smashed the lock apart. It took a few tries—I wasn't exactly sober myself. I was terrified the noise would bring people running, but Cedar Springs was sound asleep.

I woke the Stranger up though, obviously. He didn't seem surprised that someone had defied Old Margaret. He lay in bed, not shouting for help but not talking either. I asked him questions, but he politely refused to answer. I threatened him with Jack's baton, but he said nothing. I went and got Jack's gun, but that didn't scare him either. Then I broke down and cried, telling him about my wife in-between sobs. That got to him.

We talked until dawn. He told me everything. What had happened, why we were here, why drones skulked across the skies. I remembered all the friends and family I'd left behind, all my hopes and dreams, all that could have been. I remembered what life was supposed to be.

I had to leave with the sunrise. I stumbled out of the clinic, my mind shattered. I should have gone fishing, but instead I returned to my cabin and drank myself into oblivion. I awoke to the sound of the police banging on my door, each knock splitting my head like an axe. I let them in just to stop the pain.

Old Margaret's punishment was to move me from fishing to mining, a gruelling and dangerous task. She could have done much worse, but I think she showed mercy after seeing what my talk with the Stranger had done to me. And I served as a warning to Cedar Springs, a walking reminder that Old Margaret knows best.

The Stranger left in the night. A few people tried to follow his tracks, reasoning he would bring them to some form of civilisation. Adam and Jack were among them, the latter having received his own punishment for being duped. He didn't really want to go, but was too ashamed to stay. I watched them leave, but couldn't look Jack in the eye.

I think I would have joined the exodus, had I not learned what I learned. My new memories of my old life soon faded beneath the buzz of drones, but a sense of unease remained. I don't eat or sleep much anymore.

Life returned to what passes for normal in Cedar Springs. We stopped talking about the Stranger and the departed, knowing we would never see them again. After a while it was as if they had never existed.

Sometimes, when it's quiet, I can remember what the world was like before moving to Cedar Springs. It's quiet too often now. The drones only show up a few times a day, leaving me with memories that bring tears to my eyes. So I think I'll leave Cedar Springs, and walk through the trees until I remember nothing.

Snow Men

It was snowing. And not soft, fluffy, "perfect for snowmen, tobogganing and general frolic" snow. It was the grey, dreary, "let's close the curtains, make hot chocolate, huddle under the blankets and dream of summer" variety. To say nothing of the wind (which was cold), the temperature (which was low), and the hour (which was late). It was the kind of winter night where everyone stays inside.

Peter Munday was outside and not happy about it. The cold had numbed his hands, frozen his ears and reddened his nose. It had seeped through his many layers and chilled his very bones. It had forced him to redefine his understanding of the word "cold." He wanted to be home with his parents. He wanted a cup of hot chocolate more than any boy in history had ever wanted one.

But he wouldn't be getting hot chocolate, because Peter was lost. More than lost, really. Spectacularly, hopelessly, "tell the search party not to get their hopes up" lost. If there was a contest for getting lost being held at that moment, Peter wouldn't win because he wouldn't be able to find it. That's how lost he was.

It wasn't Peter's fault he was lost. When he left his friend's house he knew where he was going. But that had been hours ago, when the snow was a mere inconvenience. As he walked it had grown from an inconvenience into a nuisance, and then into a full-fledged bother. From there it soon became a problem, and now "catastrophe" was an understatement.

Peter wasn't aware it was the worst snowstorm the city had seen in a century, but he wouldn't have been surprised if you told him. It was so thick he was all but blind. The drifts were halfway to his knees, making every step a struggle. The howling wind sounded like it came from another world. All that should explain why Peter was shocked when he walked right into a girl making snowmen.

She didn't seem to mind, or even notice. But Peter noticed her. He noticed she looked his age, that she had blonde hair down to her waist, and that her eyes were the most beautiful blue he had ever seen. He also noticed she was wearing nothing but a thin grey dress. That's actually what he noticed first, which was understandable given the circumstances. Peter said the only thing he could think to say in such a strange situation.

"Hi."

"Oh, hello," said the girl, glancing at Peter before returning to her work.

"What are you doing?"

"Making snowmen."

"Aren't you cold?"

"No."

Peter felt ridiculous. And he felt ridiculous about feeling ridiculous, because he wasn't the one making snowmen in the middle of a blizzard. He wanted to ask the girl where her parents were, or where she lived, or why she hadn't frozen to death, but none of those questions seemed right. What did seem right was "Why are you making snowmen?"

"To guard against the snow men."

This, naturally, confused Peter further. He waited for her to elaborate, but she didn't. Peter suspected he could have stood there for hours and she wouldn't have said another word. So he asked, "What are snowmen?"

"They're what I'm making."

"No, I mean, what are snow *men*?"

The girl looked Peter in the eye. He felt warm.

"Snow men make the winter long and dreary. They feed on your loneliness, on your despair, on the sadness you feel in the dead of the bitterest nights. They corrupt winter's beauty."

"That sounds bad."

"It is." She returned to her snowmen.

Peter didn't know what she was talking about. But he did know that if he was going to be lost he didn't want to be lost alone. So he said, "Can I help?"

"If you'd like."

Peter took a close look at her snowmen. Their faces were stern, their bodies sturdy. Peter had never thought he could be intimidated by a snowman, but if he saw one of them in someone's yard he would steer clear.

He began his own, but both the snow and his hands were uncooperative. After much hard work he had assembled what could generously be called a snow blob, which was soon turned into a mere snow pile by the shrieking wind.

Peter kicked the pile in frustration and watched the girl work. Her bare hands sculpted the snow with ease. There was urgency in her movements, but also grace. In the time it had taken Peter to construct a pile she had made another Adonis.

"How did you get so good at making snowmen?"

"Practice." She began another without pausing.

"My name's Peter, by the way."

"Oh."

"What's yours?"

"Yuki."

"I'm not being much help, Yuki." Peter gestured at his sad little pile, but the girl wasn't looking. "This snow is terrible. Could you show me what you're doing?"

Peter thought he heard a sigh, but it might have just been the wind. Regardless, Yuki trudged over to give him a hand.

"You're fighting the snow," she said. "Shaping it against its will. You have to follow its lead."

Yuki grabbed Peter's hands, and suddenly he was no longer in a blizzard. He was on a tropical beach, basking in the sun and watching the clear blue waves lap on the shore. His hands were playing with… something. What it was didn't matter. He felt happier than he had ever been.

He blinked and the blizzard returned. Yuki had released him, though her warmth lingered. In front of him was the perfect base of a snowman, the kind every boy dreams of building.

"Like that," said Yuki. She returned to her work, leaving Peter gaping. The situation had officially progressed from odd to baffling.

"How did you do that?" he asked. "Make me feel warm, I mean."

"I don't know. I just did." Yuki shrugged. "You should get back to work."

Peter tried to finish his snowman. It felt important now, though he wasn't sure why. It was hard without Yuki's guidance, but he was able to mold the snow in ways that had eluded him earlier. Visions of sunny days danced through his head, and currents of heat shot through his body. Aftershocks of Yuki's touch.

He managed to build something that was far more man than blob, a snowman that would fit in at any schoolyard, playground or park. He turned to Yuki to brag, but the sight of what she had accomplished made his work look trivial.

Her snowmen had become snowsoldiers. Each held a snowweapon—a sword, an axe, a pike, even a flail. They were detailed, balanced and beautiful.

"Those are amazing!" said Peter, feeling envious on behalf of his own creation. "How did you make them? Can you teach me?"

"There's no time. They'll be here soon." The wind picked up, as if on cue. Peter swore it carried noises, whispers. They were too faint to be understood, but they chilled him more than the blizzard.

Yuki took a handful of black gems from a pouch on her dress and threw two to Peter. She used the rest to give her snowmen eyes.

Peter caught one gem, but fumbled the other. The whispers grew louder as he searched for it. Peter could pick out a few words, and they weren't pleasant. He thought he saw movement, shadows dancing in the distance, but it was so hard to see through the snow.

By the time he found the gem his hands were frozen. All traces of Yuki's warmth were gone. He shoved the gems into his snowman's head, knocking a chunk of it off as he did. It made the snowman look cross-eyed, but Peter liked it. He thought it gave him some personality, even if that personality was "simpleminded and possibly inbred."

Yuki was getting harder to see through the snow, but Peter could tell she had finished giving her snowmen eyes and had begun… speaking to them? Her mouth moved as she looked at her creations, but Peter couldn't hear the words. The wind roared, and Yuki and her snowmen vanished behind a wall of white. Peter, blind, stumbled towards where she had been. He heard icy laughter.

He wanted to run, but the cold had devoured his strength. Black shapes flickered at the edge of his vision. He felt frozen, lonely, empty. He fell. A shadow hovered over him, a gaunt figure wrapped in a cloak of black snow. It opened its mouth and brought icicle teeth to his neck.

A blur of white and the shadow was gone. A snowman stood over Peter, wielding a snowsword coated in brilliant blue ice. It offered him a hand up and, despite the insanity of the situation, he felt it would be rude not to take it. Once he was back on his feet the snowman lumbered off, and Peter was alone again.

He heard sounds of battle, or what he assumed a battle between snowmen and monsters would sound like. He searched for Yuki, telling himself he wanted to protect her but knowing deep down that he wanted her to protect him.

Peter caught glimpses of the struggle as he plowed through the snow. A snowman running one of the creatures through with a pike, shattering its cape into millions of black flakes. A creature ducking under an axe swing and decapitating a snowman with a swipe of a clawed hand. Snowman and snow man grappling, tumbling to the ground as they pummelled each other's unnatural bodies.

The snow was up to Peter's knees and continued to fall. Exhausted from pushing through it, he was on the verge of a second collapse when he heard Yuki's voice. She was shouting, rallying her frozen troops to her. Peter, cold enough to be an honorary snowman, heeded the call.

Yuki emerged out of the haze. A snow man slashed at her head, but she stepped aside with effortless grace and laid her hands on it. It disintegrated in a burst of heat.

Peter ran to her side. He wanted to ask her something, but wasn't sure what. "How did you do that?" would produce no answer he could comprehend, "Are you okay?" was too understated for a supernatural battle and "Could you please explain what's going on?" might take days to answer. So he asked the only question that seemed appropriate. "Are we winning?"

"For now."

"For now?"

"Yes. But the snow men will come back. They always come back."

Yuki sounded sad. Peter wished he could say something comforting. But he couldn't, because he was too busy yelling "Look out!"

Two snow men had emerged from the blizzard. Yuki spun around and destroyed one, but the other swung an arm and knocked her to the ground. It bared its teeth and moved in for the kill.

Peter attacked the snow man with the only available weapon. The first snowball drew its attention, while the second angered it enough to draw it away from Yuki. Peter was thrilled for the split-second before he realised he now had a monster charging at him.

A dozen plans rushed through his head, all of them a variant on "Panic, try to run and probably get killed." Then the snow man made eye contact, and everything became meaningless. Its eyes were chips of ice that froze Peter in his tracks. His knees buckled, his vision blurred. His will to live vanished. He didn't feel scared, though. He didn't feel anything. The snow man's clawed hand reached for Peter's throat. And then it was knocked to the ground.

Peter's snowman—his weaponless, armless, deformed snowman—had crashed into the monster. The snowman did all it could to keep its foe on the ground, first standing on it and then, whether by intention or incompetence, pinning the creature by falling on top of it.

The monster couldn't escape, but its one free arm tore chunks from the snowman's body. The strategy of "lay motionless on the enemy and hope for the best" did not appear to have long term potential.

It didn't need it. Another snowman, the one that had already saved Peter once, arrived and thrust its sword through the monster's head. It helped Peter's snowman up, then went to aid its master.

Peter ran to help, but paused at his now inanimate snowman. Huge gashes dotted its body, part of its head had been crushed, and an eye was missing. But it would survive, so Peter did all he could for the moment. He gave the snowman a hug.

Yuki was on her feet, though she leaned on her snowman for support. Deep cuts from the monster's claws ran across her face.

"Are you going to… live?" Again, it seemed the only appropriate question.

"Yes. I've suffered worse."

"Really? That, uh, sucks." Peter wasn't sure what the right thing to say to a badly wounded, apparently magical girl who had just won a battle against evil forces was, but he suspected that wasn't it.

"Yes."

"So… what now?"

"I rest, and fight again."

"Is that all you do?"

"Yes."

"I don't understand. I don't understand you, or what just happened, or anything else."

"You aren't supposed to. You weren't even supposed to be here."

"Oh." Peter's gaze dropped to the ground.

Yuki's voice softened. "But I'm thankful for your help. Let me guide you home."

She kissed Peter's cheek. Heat flooded his body, and he suddenly knew which way to go.

"Goodbye." Yuki and her snowman turned to leave.

"Bye! Stay safe!"

She looked back and smiled. "Don't worry. I will."

Peter watched until they vanished into the snow and the dark, then began to walk home. The storm still raged, but he didn't feel the slightest bit cold.

He returned to the battleground the next day. The snow, sparkling under the sun, was beautiful. The only landmark, and the only sign of what had occurred the previous night, was a beaten-up, half collapsed snowman. Peter repaired him, gave him a new eye, a carrot nose and a smile. He looked quite respectable, although still a little cross-eyed.

The Adventures of Super Sloth

You're too young to remember, but let me tell you, it was a big deal when people first started getting powers. Folks who could make their pinkie disappear or hover an inch above the ground figured it was only a matter of time before they were turning invisible or soaring through the sky. Problem was, the invisible pinkie was as good as most of us got. Neat party trick, but not so handy for fighting crime.

A few people were lucky enough to get powers you could actually call super. They were punching through steel, shooting lasers out of their eyes, you know what I'm talking about. We thought we had real superheroes to look up to, that they'd stop all the crime and capture all the terrorists and bring us all the ice cream.

And they would've been happy to do it, but the government decided they were more interested in studying these supers than letting them fight crime. I can see where they were coming from. Given the choice between letting some yahoo from West Virginia run around New York City shooting eye lasers at pickpockets, or finding out what made his super-peepers tick and giving them to Navy SEALs, well, I know what I'd choose. The government forgot one little thing, though—it's damn hard to arrest superheroes.

Most supers, facing God knows how many years of being poked and prodded in some secret lab, decided that a life of crime suddenly looked pretty appealing. Especially since, you know, there were no superheroes to stop them. Whoops.

Yeah, so that explains that little blip in crime stats. Thankfully, most of them were content to just rob a few banks and retire to private islands. But a few were crazy enough to go full out supervillain and, well, you know how that ended.

But you wanted to hear how Grandma factored into all this. Now, most people with "mundane" powers used them to impress drunk girls at bars or keep themselves from getting bored at the ol' nine to five. But I said to hell with that. When I was a girl I read comics and dreamed of getting superpowers. Just because my dream came true in the lamest way possible it didn't mean I couldn't go around helping people. So I formed the New York City League of Subpar Heroes. Get it? Ah, it was funny at the time.

We liked to think of ourselves as an oddball detective agency. We weren't planning on stopping supervillains, but we were more than happy to track down your stolen jewellery or catch your spouse cheating on you. We even solved the odd kidnapping. Yeah, we mostly just found lost pets and helped you figure out who dinged your car in the parking lot, but every bit helps, right?

So, what was my mighty power? Precognition. Sounds great, right? Just think of Spider-Man's spider sense—he can sense things before they happen and react accordingly. Well, I can sense things before they happen too, buuut I can't move fast enough to do anything about it. Real handy, huh? It's more annoying than useful, to be honest. I had to quit my dodgeball league, because I could predict when someone was going to throw a ball at me but couldn't do anything except stand there with a stupid look on my face and get smacked. So I called it sloth sense. That made me Super Sloth. Yeah, I know, not very creative. But it makes you picture a sloth wearing a cape, and that's freaking adorable. Don't tell me you can imagine it without feeling all warm and fuzzy inside.

You're probably wondering how sloth sense could be used to fight crime, and that's a fair question. Well for starters, most of our cases didn't require powers at all. You don't need x-ray vision to coax a cat out of a tree. For the gigs where our skills actually came in handy, that's where my sidekick came in.

I had a couple dozen Subpar Heroes on the books, and we teamed up for the tough jobs. You'd be amazed how many mundane powers suddenly become useful when you find ways to combine them. The Caped Cursive Reader and the Tremendous Typist, for example. Cursie could decipher even the most incomprehensible handwriting, but his typing skills were atrocious. T.T., on the other hand, was borderline illiterate, but he's the fastest damn typist I've ever seen. 200 words per minute, I swear to God. He was useless at anything else, but plop him in front of a keyboard and you'd witness a true marvel. Libraries paid good money to get messy old manuscripts digitised, and the two of them were pretty much solely responsible for keeping the League solvent in its early years. It's a damn shame they let the success go to their heads. Their reality show didn't do so hot.

Anyway, my sidekick was a girl who went by Miss Cleo. Sweet little thing, still a teenager. Helped out at the League after school. She was a precog too, but she could see what happened to *other* people. The only catch was that what she saw never happened.

Confused? I'll explain with dodgeball again, because damn, I miss that game. Say Cleo saw me getting pegged in the head, okay? Well, if she warned me, the one thing I could count on was that my head was safe. I might get hit in the chest, the ball might miss me, or it might spontaneously combust. I'm not saying that last one's plausible, but it's still *more* possible than me getting hit in the head, because that's what Cleo saw.

So we took our two useless powers and teamed up. Cleo would tell me what wasn't going to happen, and I would do my damndest to make it so. Like, this one time, we helped break up a bar fight. Some drunk was waving a knife around, and Cleo saw me get stabbed. Therefore, I *wasn't* going to get stabbed. That was *just* enough information for me to actually do something with my vision, sort of.

Obviously, then, I threw myself right at this drunk's knife. Because I knew that whatever vision *I* saw would deal with me avoiding the blade, I was kind of able to anticipate what was going to happen. I knew I would have to dodge, or duck, or remember that I put on body armour that morning and then forgotten about it.

So as I was throwing myself at this knife—which looked pretty damn sharp, mind you—I got a vision of myself juking right to avoid it. So I dodged right... and slammed into a cement wall. When I came round, Cleo told me the impact looked so vicious that everyone freaked out, stopped fighting, and called an ambulance. The crisis brought them together, and whatever petty issue started the fight was forgotten.

Yeah, it's a stupid way to fight crime. I usually didn't even do anything useful, but sloths aren't useful at all. Hence me being Super Sloth.

There you go. Super Sloth and Miss Cleo, crime fighters extraordinaire. I'll have you know that figuring out our system was *not* fun. If someone had made a training montage, ninety percent of it would be me getting hit with blunt objects. Talk about being disillusioned with your childhood dreams.

And before you ask, no, we didn't wear costumes. Why? First of all, because no self-respecting crime fighter wears costumes. Don't believe what you see in the movies, kid. They're gaudy, they get in the way and they draw attention. If you find yourself in a shootout with the Mob, do you want to be wearing neon orange? Might as well have a bull's-eye painted on you. And even if you ignored all that, what the hell were we supposed to dress as? Was I supposed to throw on a sloth costume? Where would you even find one? I sure wasn't about to *make* one. And no teenage girl would be caught dead dressing as a hotline psychic. She'd never live it down at school. So no, no costumes.

Most of our adventures weren't exactly the sort to make comic books fly off the shelves. I once stopped a murder by taking a bullet to the crotch. Cleo saw that me dodging in front of the target wouldn't kill me and, well, she was right. And we stopped a drug smuggling operation by making a school bus crash into the smugglers' truck. People were pissed about that one. Don't see why—all those broken bones mended just fine.

Our specialty was putting an end to small time gangs. We weren't taking on career criminals, just wayward kids who needed to be scared straight. I'd challenge a troublemaker to a fight, Cleo would yell out the not-future, and several serious head wounds for the both of us later the kid rethought his life of crime.

I still remember my all-time favourite bust. It was some college kid selling drugs at an abandoned construction site. He pulled brass knuckles, and Cleo said he would wallop me if I tried to dodge left, so left I went. I slipped on a patch of oil and fell into him, and we hit the ground all tangled up. My head snapped a rickety scaffold support in half, and through a concussed haze I saw the whole thing fall down on one side. An empty bucket started rolling down from the top, and just as this punk manages to stand up it plops right on his head. So he's running around threatening to kill us with a bucket stuck on him, and while he's trying to take it off he falls into a pit and knocks himself cold. Good times.

I'll put aside my wide variety of head wounds for now, because I know the story you really want to hear. Besides, recalling too many at once makes my brain hurt. Literally. So like I was saying, most so-called supervillains were really just glorified bank robbers. Even the crazy ones eventually started toning it down, because you can only hold the world hostage from a hollowed out volcano so many times before it gets a little blasé.

But this one fellow, the Frozen Fury, just wouldn't give it a rest. I don't think he was even in it for the money, he just loved the spotlight. A real attention hog, that one. He once threatened to freeze an *ice palace,* for God's sake. Nobody even knew how that would *work,* but the media ate it up anyway.

As you can guess, he could freeze water. Manipulate it too, send icicles flying and crap like that. Nasty business. He hadn't been heard from in a while—rumour was he had been trying to show off and gave himself a nasty case of frostbite—and he wanted to come back with a bang.

So he strolled into the Empire State Building in full costume. Most supervillains wore costumes, because egomania and good taste rarely go hand in hand. The Frozen Fury looked like an unusually violent figure skater. He sealed the exits with ice, put all the civilians in an ice cage and built himself a little throne room at the top of the tower. He threatened to start freezing people's blood unless… you know, I don't even remember what he wanted. The building renamed after him, maybe? Whatever, not important.

Miss Cleo and I just happened to be on the premises. And we just happened to have our ice skates with us, because it was winter and we were going to go skating later. Can you see where this is going? We ducked into the ladies' room as soon as Mr. Fury made his presence known, because what supervillains have in maniacal power they tend to lack in common sense. Old F.F. had a very childlike "If I can't see them, they don't exist," mindset, so he never thought to look around for errant hostages. Or maybe he just didn't want to go into the girl's room. Who knows?

The elevators had been frozen out of commission, so Cleo and I hoofed it up the stairs. And between you and me, that was the hardest part of the whole damn adventure. Be you superhero, subpar hero or regular old schmuck, climbing the Empire State Building will take it out of you. And you don't look very heroic when you burst into a villain's lair panting and sweating like a pig.

But we made it to Fury's little throne room, skates strapped on because, as predicted, the whole place was covered in ice. There were icicles that could kill a man dangling from the ceiling, and an elaborate ice throne for Fury to sit on. Must've been cold.

He did the whole evil speech thing—he loved giving speeches—while Cleo and I skated in little circles because we weren't very good at standing still on blades. We kind of tuned Fury out, but it was something about how we would rue the day, and how he would freeze us solid and bring New York to its knees, and also there were a lot of lousy water and ice puns. Supervillains love their puns. Don't ask me why, I don't know.

Cleo saw me charging the throne, tripping like an idiot, and cracking my head open. Being a poor skater I was concerned that this would be the one vision that came true, but nevertheless I lunged right at the Frozen Fury like a homicidal Michelle Kwan. Fury started dropping his killer icicles on us while shouting something about how we were going to have ice water in our veins. Poor Cleo had to rely on actual reflexes to dodge them, but she was a better skater than me, so she held her own. I just did my best to ignore them and keep on trucking, although the fact that getting speared by one was an open possibility made that a little difficult.

I was almost at the throne when it hit me—I saw myself going into a slide to avoid a crack in the ice. Not really expecting that as a possibility, I was barely able to throw myself down in time. But I did it, and it hurt like a mother. I went flying out of control, blades first, towards the Frozen Fury.

Fury, not relishing the prospect of getting skates buried three inches into his shins, scampered out of the way... and right into the path of one of his falling icicles. I'll spare you the gory details. Let's just say that while he survived, he wasn't in any shape to fight back. I, meanwhile, got my skates stuck in his stupid throne. And since the icicle hanging right above my chest was on the brink of snapping off I thought I had to make a last second getaway, just like my comic book heroes.

Unfortunately, fumbling at skate laces with frozen fingers isn't exactly up there with outrunning an explosion. I eventually had to give up and just scoot over a little so the icicle came crashing down next to me. It wasn't even a last second scoot. I had to sit there for like a minute waiting for the stupid thing to fall. Riveting, right?

But you didn't hear that part—Cleo and I punched the story up a bit when we were telling it to the cops. Sure, the Frozen Fury disputed us, but who was going to believe him? One of the downsides of being a supervillain is that you're not considered trustworthy.

Well, you know the rest of the story. Fury went to one of those secret government labs he had been trying to avoid, and Cleo and I were heroes. We did lots of interviews, we were awarded the key to the city, we were even guests on *The Tonight Show*. We did a bit where I used our powers to stop Jimmy Fallon from slapping me. Unfortunately, I did it by making an overhead light fall on him, and that's when our star began to fade.

Business at the League boomed for a while, but then another supervillain foiling took the headlines and we faded back into obscurity. And that's fine with me, because as much as I loved my comic books, they sure made being a hero look easier than it really is. Now, would you be a dear and go get me my hot water bottle? I see that this rickety old chair is finally about to give out on me, and I don't have time to—

Ow. Son of a bitch.

The Clones of Tehran

Drones buzzed overhead as Miller entered the restaurant. The front looked normal enough, but the back half was a mess of rubble and blood. Policemen collected evidence and took statements as paramedics carried out bodies covered in white sheets. Miller flashed his badge at the soldier who greeted him and walked over to a pair of policeman chatting in the corner.

"Well, if it isn't my favourite buddy cop duo."

"Miller." Ezra, the taller of the two, offered his hand. The short, perpetually scowling Ali merely nodded.

"How many this time?"

"We're still scraping bits and pieces off the ceiling, but at least twenty. Mostly civilians, plus a couple IDF on patrol."

"Any ideas on a motive, besides the usual troublemaking?"

"The owner is related to one of the bigshots in the Transitional Government," said Ali. "But he wasn't in the restaurant today."

"Wouldn't be the first time they've acted on shoddy intel."

Miller pursed his lips as he glanced around the remains of the building. This was, what, the third bombing this week? Fourth? At least it wasn't as bad as the mosque. Shame, though. He had always meant to eat here.

"Another vatman?" he said.

"Do you even have to ask?"

"No need to get snippy, Ali. Let me know when your tech boys have figured out what the bomb was made of. I want to know how they got past the sensors *this* time."

"A witness said he saw the host slip out the door right after the bomber came in," said Ezra. "We're thinking he was bribed to disable the sensors."

"Find him, fast. Shouldn't be hard for Tehran's finest, right?"

Neither of the men looked amused by Miller's joke. He made a mental note not to try another one just as his ear buzzed.

"Miller? It's Browning."

"What's up, Chris?"

"The police have a guy they're pretty sure has a connection to the Guard. They're holding him for us."

"Is 'pretty sure' more or less sure than when they were 'really sure' about that student being a Guard agent?"

"Come on, just get down here. I just had to listen to another lecture from Langley, and that was before they heard about the latest bomb."

"Alright, I'm on my way." To the policemen he said, "Duty calls, gentlemen. I take it you know the drill by now?"

They nodded and went back to picking through the rubble. Miller walked back out into the beautiful spring evening, taking care not to step in any blood on the way.

***

Light, muffled sounds. Blobs moving on the other side. He was used to all this. But the sounds were louder now, the blobs closer. Suddenly, the liquid that suspended him began to drain away. He felt his feet touch something cold, heard a crack and a hiss. The other side was coming to him. He was scared.

A door swung away and a blob took shape. It looked like him. The man offered him his hand. He hesitantly took it.

"Hello, Navid. My name is Yousef."

"I am... Navid?"

The man smiled. "Yes. Yes you are."

***

The interrogation room was cramped and grimy. A paunchy middle-aged man, head drooped, was tied to a wooden chair in the centre. Behind him were two policemen, their faces blank. Browning stood by the door. Leaning against the wall was Simon, the Mossad man.

"What do we got, Browning?" asked Miller.

"This is Saeed. Runs a bakery near the school that was bombed last week."

"Yeah? His bread any good?"

"Beats me."

Miller lifted the man's head up. His face was battered and bruised, his nose broken. The fear in his deep brown eyes made Miller think of the deer he used to hunt back home.

"Christ, Simon, what did you do to him?"

"We were just getting to know each other." Simon grinned.

"Do you actually think this guy's with the Guard, or were you just looking for an excuse to beat up some locals?"

Simon's smile vanished. "Don't tell me how to do my job, Miller."

Miller saw the policemen exchange a glance.

"Alright, Simon, I'll show you how."

Miller lifted the prisoner's head up again. He took a cloth from his pocket and wiped the blood from the man's nose. In Farsi he said, "Hey, Saeed. My name's Miller. We're going to have a little chat."

"I didn't do anything." Saeed's voice was ragged.

"I'd like to believe that, but you've got to convince me. You have any friends in the Guard?" Miller crouched down to Saeed's level.

"No. I don't want trouble."

"Come on, you're an older guy. No buddies from before the war you've been staying in touch with?"

"My 'buddies' were killed in the invasion."

"You sound a little bitter, Saeed."

"No! No, I don't want any problems."

Miller glanced back at Simon. "You have any motives for this guy, or are you just wasting my time?"

"Money. Our baker is in debt, and his creditors are… impatient."

"That true, Saeed? You having money troubles?"

"People are afraid to go outside and shop. I had to take a loan to keep my bakery open." The man had calmed down a little when Miller started talking to him, but now he was nervous again.

"Must be tough to pay back a loan when the economy's in shambles. But I hear the Guard pays well for help…"

"I would never work with them! Please, I swear."

"Saeed, what's the name of the man you owe money to?"

"Karim. He's a thug, but I was desperate."

Miller stood and addressed the policemen. "What was the name of the guy who tipped you off?"

"Karim, sir," said the Iranian one.

"So our suspect owes money to a man named Karim, and you roughed him up because a man named Karim told you he might be a terrorist. Great fucking detective work, guys. Really impressive stuff." Miller clapped as the policemen dropped their gaze. "Hey, Simon, I thought you were supposed to be teaching these guys not to be such dumbasses."

Simon glared at Miller, then the police.

"Come on, Chris, let's get out of here." Miller left the room.

***

Navid liked Yousef. Yousef was a nice man who was teaching Navid a lot. He told Navid that they were both people called Iranians, and that they could not go outside because people called Americans and Israelis were trying to kill Iranians. But Yousef taught Navid how to behave for when they were allowed to go outside. He showed Navid pictures and videos of what outside looked like. Outside looked nice. Yousef also showed Navid pictures of Americans and Israelis. They looked mean. Navid didn't like those pictures.

Navid did like his brothers. They all looked just like Navid, though their names were different. Yousef was teaching them too. He said that one day, hopefully soon, they would all get to go outside. Navid liked to talk with his brothers about what outside might be like, though Yousef didn't like it when they talked without him. He said that would put silly ideas in their heads. Navid didn't understand, but he obeyed. He trusted Yousef.

Navid didn't like Hamid. Hamid was rude to Navid and his brothers. He was even rude to Yousef. Yousef would tell Hamid to be patient, and he would go away for a few days. But then he would come back and be rude again. He had just come for another visit, which had put Navid in a bad mood. But Yousef had just announced that he had exciting news, which made Navid happy. He couldn't wait to hear it.

***

Miller looked up from a dossier on the restaurant host Ali and Ezra had tracked down. "Take the next right," he said to Browning.

"Right? Isn't it faster to go by the university?"

"Not if you want this hunk of junk to stay in one piece. Students are protesting again."

"Again? Jesus."

Miller laughed. "What do you think of your first couple weeks in Iran, kid?"

"I think it's a mess. Half the country wants democracy, the other half wants the Ayatollah back, the Mossad doesn't want either, and none of them trust us. How the hell are we supposed to do anything?"

"Don't worry, we don't have to rebuild the place. We just need to stop the Guard from blowing people up long enough for the Israelis to slap together a government that can keep order while still kissing their ass, and then we can go home until somebody fucks things up again. So, a few months."

"Damn, Miller."

Miller laughed. "It's not that bad. We're here to save lives, and that's a good thing no matter whose side you're on. Hell of a lot better than what I had to do in Damascus. Take that left."

"You served in Damascus?"

"I don't want to talk about it."

They drove in silence the rest of the way to the police station. Miller watched a drone fly by before they entered the building.

Ezra was waiting for them at his desk. It hadn't been long since Miller last saw him, but he looked more stressed.

"Miller, Browning." He didn't offer a hand.

"Ezra. Where's your buddy?" asked Miller.

"Stakeout. Our restaurant host was… talkative."

"You don't sound convinced."

"It didn't take much to get him going. The Guard must be getting desperate if they're hiring unreliable help. Either that or he's lying. My bet's on the latter."

"Let's hope you're wrong. What did he say?"

Ezra swivelled his monitor around, showing them a photo of a house. "Says the Guard have been operating out of here." The address indicated it wasn't far from the station.

"Looks big enough to hold a cloning lab," said Browning. "But how could they suck up that much power without drawing suspicion?"

"There are ways to mask consumption," said Miller. "Still, they'd have to have some serious balls to run a lab just outside the Green Zone."

"Hiding in plain sight, I guess. I don't buy it, though," said Ezra.

"I take it this is what Ali's checking out?"

"Yeah, he's keeping an eye on it. Hasn't reported anything unusual yet, though."

"Guess we should pay a visit. Thanks, Ezra."

Miller and Browning stood to go. Ezra was already on the phone, learning about the latest problem.

***

Navid was very happy. He had been wondering why he had not seen some of his brothers recently, and now he knew it was because they had gone outside! He asked Yousef when they would come back, and was sad to hear that they were too busy outside to come and visit. But he cheered up when he was told that soon he would get to go outside too. He had already been allowed to leave their home—Yousef had brought him into what he knew was called a van. He was in the back of the van, so he couldn't see outside, but he enjoyed being bumped up and down and side to side as they moved. But the van hadn't moved for quite some time, and Navid was getting lonely—none of his brothers were with him. Yousef had promised that he would be back soon, and that once Navid went outside he would be reunited with his brothers. So Navid waited patiently, smiling as he imagined the wonderful things his brothers would tell him.

***

Miller and Browning slipped into the backseat of Ali's car. Ali was looking out the window with a pair of smart specs and, to Miller's annoyance, Simon was with him.

"I was wondering when you two would show up," said Simon. He removed his specs and handed them to Miller. "Have a look."

Miller slipped the glasses on. The house at the end of the street zoomed into view.

"Looks normal enough. What do you think, Ali? You've been here a while." Miller gave the specs to Browning.

"I think we're wasting our time. It's been a bit busy, but nothing suspicious."

"I disagree," said Simon. "I had a chat with a few of the neighbours. 'A bit busy' would be a severe understatement."

"Alright, well, keep watching it and we'll see what happens," said Miller. "Sound good to you, Ali?"

"Just perfect."

"We can't afford to sit around and wait. By the time our suspicions are confirmed there will be another bombing," said Simon.

"So what, you want to send a team in?" asked Miller.

"Forget it," said Ali. "We're not sending police in there. Do you have any idea how many traps the Guard will have set up?"

Simon swore. "Fine, then I'll call it in. But don't blame me if it gets messy."

"You want to use a drone? In the middle of a suburb?" Ali removed his specs and stared at Simon. "Are you crazy? Come on, Miller, back me up here."

"You sure about this, Simon?"

"Very."

Miller and Browning exchanged a look.

"Your call, boss. I'm just the new guy."

"Fuck you, Chris." Miller sighed. He thought of the restaurant and the mosque, and the men back home demanding results. "Alright. Hit it."

Simon got on the phone and said a few words in Hebrew. Then they waited.

It didn't take long. There was a buzz, a boom, a flash. When the dust cleared they saw that the house had turned to rubble. Miller heard a few screams, but he had learned to tune those out long ago.

The men got out and walked down the road, passing fleeing civilians as they went. They found bodies in the wreckage, a man and a girl that had been crushed by the collapsing second storey. Blood and body parts suggested others in the house had been caught in the explosion.

"Shit," said Ali. "I told you."

"If your men weren't jumping at shadows we wouldn't have to resort to this," said Simon.

The men glared at each other. Miller worried it would come to blows, but Browning relieved the tension by calling them over.

"Basement's over here." He pulled out a penlight and shone it down the stone steps.

"Let's have a look." Miller led them down and flashed his own light around. The shock of the strike had made a mess, but his eye still caught things that were out of place. Someone had left in a hurry.

Simon plucked a fluid sack from the ground and waved it in Ali's face. "You told me, huh? Look familiar?" It was the liquid used to sustain gestating vatmen.

"You think that's proof? Where's the rest of the lab?"

"Oh, shit," said Miller. "It's mobile."

"What?" Simon wheeled around to face Miller.

"Their labs are mobile. They make a vatman, break the lab down and scatter the pieces, then reassemble in a different location. Hell, they could even be making them in stages."

"That would explain how they're masking their power use," said Browning. "If they only spike the power for a day or two, it wouldn't be enough to arouse suspicion."

"Hell, they could even be running on generators. And they could be sneaking into houses when the owners are gone, bribing or threatening people for an overnight stay, calling in favours... Jesus."

"If you're right, this means a complete change in tactics. We'll need to start searching cars too."

"We're already stretched thin," said Simon.

"Well, we don't exactly have a choice."

Ali had wandered off to take a call, and now rejoined the group. "That was Ezra. You're going to want to hear this."

***

Navid was so excited, not even the presence of Hamid could dampen his spirits. He was going to go outside! The van was moving again, and Yousef was giving him instructions as Hamid fitted a vest on him. It was a little bulky, but Navid didn't mind.

Yousef was telling him that he would see some Americans and Israelis when he went outside, but he needed to be nice to them. He asked Yousef if they would try to kill him, and Navid said they wanted to, but couldn't. He asked why, but Yousef told him to stop asking questions. He was a little rude to Navid, which was unlike him, but Navid thought he was just sad to see him leave.

Hamid put something in Navid's hair and eyes that changed their colour. As he did this, Yousef told Navid what he had to do outside. They were going to let Navid out near a restaurant, and Navid was to go in and order some food. Yousef told him to enjoy his food until a man—Yousef showed him a picture—arrived. This man was a friend of Yousef's, and Navid was to go over and introduce himself. He was then supposed to press a button on his vest, which would let Yousef know the man was there. Then Yousef would come and tell him what to do next.

Yousef kept repeating his instructions, but for the first time in his life Navid ignored him. He was too busy wondering what he would be able to eat at the restaurant.

***

Miller sipped his tea as he watched people enter the restaurant. Simon sat across from him, toying with his food. The presumed target of the last restaurant bombing was visiting his other two establishments, to ease the concerns of jittery workers. Miller couldn't decide if the man was very brave or very foolish, but either way he was a target. As they looked for vatmen here, Browning and Ali were across town doing the same.

Miller had seen army and labour vatmen, and he'd seen what was left of the corpses of the vatmen the Guard were using, but he'd never had to pick out a live bomber. He looked for single diners, or pairs of men that were suspiciously similar. But the Guard were good at disguising their operatives, and that sent his heart racing whenever someone so much as dropped a fork.

He had his eyes on one man sitting in the corner, and a pair not far from him. Simon, looking in the other direction, had his own targets. Their table in the centre of the room gave them a view of the entire restaurant, but it also meant they would be caught in a blast no matter where it came from.

"There's our VIP," said Simon. The owner had arrived. Miller wrapped his hand around the gun hidden under his jacket.

***

Navid was having the time of his life. Outside was loud and confusing, but by sitting in the corner of the restaurant and watching the world go by he was starting to get a grip on it. He gave a friendly smile to anyone who looked at him and, to his great satisfaction, most people smiled back. Even the Americans and Israelis were being friendly. That confused him, but maybe they had been told to pretend to be nice just like he had been.

Navid especially liked his food. It was far better than what Yousef had fed him, although he wouldn't tell him that. He didn't want to hurt Yousef's feelings. He didn't even know what he was eating was called. Overwhelmed by the menu, he had asked the waiter to bring him the tastiest food the restaurant had. That had amused the waiter. Navid raved about how much he loved his meal whenever the waiter came to check on him, and that made the waiter very happy. He would have to ask the waiter what it was called.

The man in the picture entered the restaurant. Navid tensed— this was his chance to prove to Yousef that he could be trusted. This was his chance to prove that he belonged outside.

He let the man and his companions get settled as he thought about how best to approach him. When he decided, he stood up and walked to the man's table. He was so excited that he walked very quickly.

Another man, an American, got up and blocked Navid's path. He spoke to Navid in a deep voice.

"Hey. What's your name?"

This American was not pretending to be nice like the others. He sounded stern yet nervous, like he didn't trust Navid. Navid didn't like this man, but he remembered Yousef's instructions and responded politely.

"I'm Navid."

"Hello, Navid. My name's Miller."

"It's a pleasure to meet you, Miller."

"What are you doing here today, Navid?"

"I'm just enjoying a meal." That was what Yousef told Navid to say if anyone questioned him.

"Oh yeah? You seem to be in a hurry to go somewhere."

"I saw a friend. If you would please excuse me, I would like to talk to him." Navid tried to step around the American, but the man did not relent.

"What's your friend's name, Navid?"

"I'm sorry, I must go speak with him." Yousef had not told Navid the name of his friend. The American was making Navid very nervous.

"What's the rush? I'd like to ask you a few things." The American put his hand on Navid's shoulder. He was smiling now, trying to look friendly, but he didn't fool Navid.

"I…" Yousef had not told Navid what to do if this happened. He was getting worried.

"How did you get here, Navid?"

"A… a friend drove me." Navid decided to be honest with the American. All Yousef wanted Navid to do was say hello to a friend. There was nothing wrong with that. If the American realised that, he would have no reason to distrust him.

"A friend, huh? Did your friend ask you to do anything while you were here?"

"He told me to say hello to his friend."

"Yeah? Anything else?"

"He told me to press a button." Navid opened his jacket to show the American his vest. He saw a man behind the American point something at him, and then he saw nothing at all.

***

"Jesus Christ, Simon!" Miller wiped blood and brains from his shirt. "I was trying to bring him in alive!"

There was panic in the restaurant. People ran or hit the ground while soldiers rushed in to control the situation.

Simon kicked the vatman to make sure he was dead. "He was going for the trigger."

"Bullshit. He was answering my questions. I had him under control."

"You don't know that."

"The hell I don't. Weren't you listening to us?"

"I wasn't about to risk the lives of everyone in here so you could have a chat with a terrorist vatman."

"Do you have any idea how valuable a live one would be to us?"

Before Simon could respond the restaurant's owner, pale-faced and trembling, asked them for an explanation of what just happened. Miller left Simon to answer. He stepped outside and watched a drone soar overhead.

Afterword

Hi! Thanks for making it this far, assuming you didn't just skip ahead to the Afterword like a weirdo. If you've enjoyed what you've read, please consider leaving a review and telling your friends, both of which help tremendously. If you didn't enjoy what you've read, then I appreciate you making it this far anyway. That was very sporting of you.

If this collection sells well, which in this context means I can buy mid-range beer with the profits instead of the cheap stuff, I will probably work on a collection of brand new stories in-between my other obligations. If it doesn't even sell well enough to recuperate the cost of the cover art then I'll probably never mention this collection again, passionately deny its existence whenever I'm confronted about it, and allow these stories to become lost again. You will remember them only like you remember a fevered dream, and you'll begin to wonder if they were ever truly real at all.

Either way, thanks for reading and supporting this project. Short stories are creatively rewarding but often not financially rewarding, and the fact that you were willing to spend a few dollars helps negate that problem and significantly increases the odds that I'll be able to make more for the continued amusement of us both. If you'd like to read more from me in the meantime I'm an editor and columnist at Cracked.com and a sporadic contributor to many other sites, a list of which I maintain alongside some personal work at www.mehill.org. I guess that covers everything. Goodbye.

20557932R00062

Printed in Poland
by Amazon Fulfillment
Poland Sp. z o.o., Wrocław